INTERNAL AFFAIRS

Makenzi

ACKNOWLEDGEMENTS

I'm so thankful to God for giving me life and the ability to write.

To those who support me, thank you for wishing me the best. It never goes unnoticed.

Thank you to everyone who contributed to my success, my editor, test readers, book cover designer, friends, writing peers and mere acquaintances. The feedback pushes me to the next level with my writing.

To everyone that's living with a dream, never give up on that dream. Just because of the time it may take to accomplish your dream doesn't mean it will never happen.

Much love,

Makenzi

CHAPTER ONE

Ja'Shay

Cringing at the sharp pain shooting through my head, I slowly opened my eyes. It felt like the worst headache ever. After lying still for a good minute, praying for the pain to subside, I rolled over onto something wet and warm. Slowly sitting up, I looked down at the open tube of K-Y Jelly, its contents soaked into the cotton sheets. I flinched at the muscular frame lying next to me, with his back toward me and the sheet pulled up just at top of his waist, exposing the small of his back.

"*Who is—*" I mouthed, stopping short when I realized we weren't in my bed. I looked around the well-furnished, tan-colored room, with the soft, king-sized bed. Early morning sunlight peeking through the opening of brown curtains drawn across a large window, as I immediately lay back down because of the sharp pounding on the left side of my head. I placed my cool palm on my forehead, hoping this would help. Perplexity about this dude lying next to me added to the continuous pounding in my head.

The stranger shifted in his sleep, and I self-consciously pulled the sheet up to my neck.

Wait a second, why am I naked?

Panic was setting in. I pulled back the sheet, revealing both our nakedness. I released a soft, but high-pitched shrill, as I looked over at the stranger. Leaning in a little closer for a better look, I stared at his bare backside, with my mouth hanging wide open in shock.

Oh, shit! Oh, shit! Oh, shit!

My rapid beating heart replaced the shooting pain in my head. The man sleeping so peacefully next to me was Glen, a manager at my job! Unexplainable thoughts whirled around in my head, unable to piece anything together. I groaned inwardly.

What happened last night?

As I lay naked next to Glen, I reminisced, relived, and replayed in my head events from last night. I remember Glen had suggested a couple of coworkers meet at the bar where the majority of us spent our time at after work. Opened late, the bar drew a crowd closer to my age, and it hosted local bands. It had been a while since we'd gone out as a group where we were able to sit down and relax together. Glen, Lynette, Cynthia, Derrick, Trina, Ahmad, Clarence, Kelly, and I were sitting at a wooden table, talking about our lives outside of work.

"Excuse me. Can we get another round this way?" Glen had asked the server.

Three hours later, I realized Glen had bought the table several rounds of drinks, and I had one too many of those drinks. It was starting to get a little late and I still had a thirty-minute drive from the bar to my apartment. I wanted to make a graceful exit without making a fool out of myself, but wasn't sure how that would be possible, since the alcohol had gotten the best of me. In my attempt to stand up and leave the bar, I stumbled on the chair leg and toppled backward into Glen's lap.

"I'll help you to your car," Glen had said.

Thank goodness, it is him and not Clarence, who always smells like cigarettes.

Trying to shake the embarrassment, I yelled, *"Glen, I am not a fucking child! I am twenty-three years old and perfectly capable of walking myself to my car."* I struggled to regain my balance, but it was too late and I was sailing toward the floor when I felt two strong, warm arms wrap around me and a deep voice in my ear.

"Well, someone's buzz has definitely been killed." I giggled a little, as he led me through the door. The cold air of the fall night hit me immediately, sobering me up a bit, regaining some semblance of my mental filter.

"You really don't have to do this, Glen." I took a step, and my ankle buckled. Glen reached out and grabbed me, stabilizing me.

"Obviously, you're not all right. Do you want me to take you home?" He smiled.

I returned the smile. *"Yeah, I think that would be a good idea."* We both laughed.

Suddenly, I heard his voice, snapping me out of my dream-like state.

"Morning," Glen sang, as he eyed my naked body, with his head propped up on the palm of his hand.

I looked down at myself and quickly pulled the sheet up to my neck, covering myself. "What?" I sat up in the bed. "I must have been really drunk."

"Yes, we both were drunk. I remember us kissing in the parking lot. And man, you can kiss, and then you asked to come to my place." A devious grin masked mouth.

I rolled my eyes. "Can we...can we forget about this? Last night?"

"Well, I certainly don't want to forget about this." He smirked.

"This is your entire fault, Glen! You got me drunk!" I exclaimed loudly.

Glen reached out to me, but I scared him off with my look.

"Ja'Shay—"

"Don't! Just don't!"

"I'm sorry, okay?"

"No! It's not okay! I...I should go home now. And, forget about this. We will forget about this." I swung my legs over the bed, placing my feet on the floor.

"Wait."

"What?" I snapped, refusing to look back at him.

"You can shower first, if you want, while I cook breakfast."

"Thanks, but no thanks."

"Come on, Ja'Shay," Glen pleaded.

"I'm going home. Now!" I rose from the bed, spun around, and shot him a look. "Turn around."

"Why?"

"Don't ask. Just turn around!"

"Fine." He rolled over, sighed heavily, and waited.

I gathered my clothes and dressed as fast as I could. "You can turn around now."

Glen rose from the bed, shaking his head.

"Glen!" I yelled, covering my eyes with my hand.

Naked as a Jaybird, he walked toward the bathroom, grinning. He returned a few minutes later wearing underwear and a night-robe. I was now standing in the hallway, preparing to make my exit.

Glen mouthed, *"Thank you."*

"I don't want to hear anything about this anymore!" I commanded, as I walked out the door.

When I arrived to my apartment, I went straight to the bedroom, where I stripped down to nothing. In the bathroom, I turned on the faucet to draw a warm bath, and added apple-scented bubble bath. I went to the kitchen for a glass of water. My head was still hurting from all the alcohol last night, but I didn't care. I just wanted to forget about what had happened between Glen and me.

With the glass of water in hand, I went back to the bathroom. I turned off the running water, placed the glass on the sink, and turned on the radio. "Drunk in Love" by Beyoncé was playing, which was so befitting of me at the moment. With deliciously warm water, I stepped into the tub and settled down. The warm water relaxed me. I closed my eyes, listening to Beyoncé croon, as I fell deep in thought about last night.

I remembered kissing Glen in the parking lot of the bar before he sat me in the passenger seat of his car.

"Take me to your place," I had said. My hormones were raging like wild fire.

There were no words on the ride to his place, except the smooth jazz oozing from the Bose speakers. The leather seat warming my behind felt like butter, as I laid my spinning head back against the headrest of his Mercedes Benz E350. I closed my eyes, to keep the car from spinning. I definitely had too much to drink.

When we arrived at his place, he escorted me inside the building and into the elevator. The ride to the fifth floor felt like an eternity, as he grabbed my hand, intertwining his fingers with mine.

The elevator doors opened. He tugged my hand and I followed him off the elevator. He looked at me, smiled, and slipped my hand inside his pocket. I looked at him, dumfounded.

"Someone wants to meet you," he had said.

"Oh," was all I could muster, as my hand brushed against the hardened tip of his penis.

Smiling devilishly, he inserted his key in the door, opened it, and stepped inside.

"Come in. Make yourself at home."

I stepped inside and he closed the door behind me. I dropped my purse and kicked off my shoes by the front door. What followed next was a whirlwind. Hungrily, he grabbed me and started kissing me, his hands roaming all over me, fondling my breasts, my waist, cupping my behind.

Hastily, we moved to his bedroom. He pressed me against the wall, pinning my arms above my head, kissing me fervently. He slowly started to undress me and, while stepping out of my jumpsuit, I worked the buttons on his shirt. Lifting me gently, he carried me to his bed, laying me down as if I were a delicate flower. He removed my bra. Then, my panties. I wrapped my legs around his waist. He leaned in and started kissing my neck, moving down to my breasts, suckling each nipple, before moving slowly to my belly until he reached my waist.

I throbbed between my thighs, as his fingers teased inside me. He played with me until I was groaning and gasping for air, my back arching. Glen pulled up away from me. He looked down at me, while his pants and boxers fell to the floor. Again, he hovered over me; his hands flanked the sides of my head. I wrapped my chocolate legs around his vanilla waist, bringing him closer. He lowered his weight on me, and kissed, again. I gasped for air when he slowly pushed inside me. Moaning and groaning, Glen's girth filled me. Moving slowly at first, he increased his momentum, giving me an incredible arousal. More pleasure than I'd ever expected or enjoyed before. With all the lust built inside us, it didn't take long to reach our first orgasm.

As Tyrese's "Shame on Me" bounced off the walls, I returned from my trip down Memory Lane. While it was a great night, maybe the best I've ever had, it was a mistake. A big mistake. Glen was my manager. I was not good enough for him. But, last night, he made my body feel great. Yet, it still wasn't right... it may have felt so, but it shouldn't have happened. But I can't change what already happened. Only time would tell where *this* would go.

CHAPTER TWO

Desiree

The Call Center was a soap opera and reality show rolled into one. I was new to the Call Center experience, thanks to my cousin, Veronica, who referred me for the position. She told me some crazy stories about people smiling in each other's faces and partying for a few weeks before falling out with each other. The women were ratchet and wore club attire, completely disregarding the dress code. People constantly gossiped about other people. Some were screwing managers; it was like an orgy, everybody fucking everybody, and someone was always pregnant. She told me one woman fucked both men *and* women on her floor *and* the floor above her. Management played favoritism, promoting those they liked and hired any and everybody, but would fire you in a heartbeat. The story that scared me from almost applying was about a woman representative who was fighting her manager, and security had to drag her out the building. I'm just scared to death of being fired. With my

13

short-tempered attitude, I might punch a supervisor in the face because of his or her mouth.

Being unemployed and unable to pay my bills, on top of a horrible job market, did not ease my tension either. Veronica did say the customers were annoying, but hilarious at times.

As I stepped out of my car, I peered at the building. It looked as if it had to be at least six hundred people that worked there. When I first applied for jobs after graduation, I was very excited, but now I'm just annoyed because I need a job badly. I've lost count of the number of applications I've submitted.

I understood that finding a job in my field after graduating would not be immediate, so I didn't see a need to put too much pressure on myself or take a job where I would inevitably hate working. Working at the Call Center to be temporary, to cover my expenses until I figured out what I wanted to do with myself, and this Bachelor of Science in Health Sciences degree I earned from Old Dominion University.

My heels clicked on the pavement, eliciting an echo throughout the parking lot. My stomach was in knots; I felt as if I would pass out at any minute.

Inhaling, the cool morning air filled my lungs. I was startled out of my thoughts by the sound of someone loudly slamming a car door.

"What the *fuck!* That scared the shit out of me," I blurted, as I continued to walk toward the entrance.

Walking inside lobby, I forced a smile at the receptionist. She was quite pretty and seemed nice enough. She was tall, with bright brown eyes, slightly dark in complexion; she looked to be Ethiopian. She was wearing a blue fitted shirt over skinny jeans. Alexandria Fletcher, the name on the badge pinned to her shirt. Her name suited her well enough.

"Hello, my name is Desiree Bryant and I have an eight-forty-five interview." I politely spoke with a fake undertone.

"Who are you meeting with?"

"The email I received said Clarence Fox."

"Okay, I will let him know you're here. Please have a seat." She pointed toward the waiting area.

I smiled, again, as I turned to walk across the room to take a seat on the couch. The lobby area was huge with off-white colored walls, dark brown carpeting, and a glossy black desk that encircled Alexandria.

Initially, I had flirted my way through a phone interview and two more in person, so I had to be patient. This, I hoped, would be the final interview. Within two minutes of the start of the interview, I knew I had the job. This Clarence Fox person was impressed that I had done my research on the company, so I got my fancy-schmancy headset and a four-week training on credit card collection, and voila! Paid to sit in a cubicle for forty hours a week and talk to customers about them owing money.

The pay was decent, but would be accounted for student loan, gas, overpriced drinks at the bar, food from the on-site cafe and a wardrobe that I maintained, so I could go to the club. Working at The Call Center is life-draining most of the time, but otherwise it's pretty cool. I hated having the same conversation fifty times a day though, and I never expected the nightmares and the paranoia. Veronica conveniently left that shit out.

Seventy-five percent of the calls were no big deal: customers calling to make payments or wanting to know why they couldn't use their credit cards. I'd get the facts, serviced the call, and sent them on their way. The other twenty-five percent got a little more of my attention: joking with a customer about how their car always broke down because it was a Ford and, yeah, I drove a reliable Honda. Listening as they berated me because they didn't pay their bill, and there's nothing I could do about them not being able to use their card while on vacation. Having a know-it-all talk down to me because they were late for a meeting and needed to get a payment processed and off the damn phone after being on hold for so long. Trying to be patient when an old woman wanted to tell me all about her cats and how much they loved the squirrels that lived out of her bird feeder, when all I needed was her bank's routing number and checking account number, so we could end the call, but she wanted to continue talking about her grown children and their families, and now that her husband had passed away, she had no one to talk to, and even though I wanted to, I couldn't hang up without being fired.

I was just waiting for someone to come into work and have a nervous breakdown. The Call Center was just a loud school cafeteria, with people swinging by your desk every fifteen minutes, while munching on something that smelled incredible, to joke with you about reality TV, Facebook, Instagram, a new movie and what you did last night, who you screwed or just flirting. Managers that graduated five seconds before you acted as if they were commander in chief and all they wanted to know was where you bought that outfit, shoes and who was on your fantasy football draft. That's when they're not at your desk with a stack of papers, questioning why it had taken you twenty minutes between starting your shift to hitting your Auto-In button.

My fingers flew over the phone as I logged in with a whole bunch of numbers that told my manager everything about me, except my shoe size. I was officially on the clock with twenty seconds to spare before I was marked for being late. Again. Third time and I was still in my ninety-day probation period.

"Damn, girl, you barely made it," Ahmad joked. Ahmad sat across the aisle and one desk back, so he had a perfect view of the back of my head every single day. Lucky him.

"Shut up," I snapped.

"Wasn't gonna say anything, but the bitch is watching." He smiled, leaning as far back as possible in his chair, waiting for a call to come in.

I turned around in my chair, coming eye-to-eye with the manager, Kelly, who was watching my every move. I pulled my keys and cell phone out of my purse, dropped them in my top desk drawer, and fired up my computer. My desk was bare, except for the desktop monitor and the phone of evil, while others around me had a few pictures here and there. Ahmad had hand drawn pictures of Beyoncé and Lil Kim hung in his cubicle, along with a framed picture of him and his boyfriend, Dave, on his desk that I think he only put up because Dave worked here and came by his desk every once in a while.

"How's it been?" I asked Ahmad, putting on my headset, as my finger hovered over the Auto-In button that I really, really didn't want to press. I glanced at him. He was lounged back, tossing up a ball and catching it.

"The usual, *'Why are you calling me on Sunday? It's the Lord's Day.'*" He laughed "But, so far it's been slow; about ten minutes between and just a bunch of customer service transfers."

"Sweet," I said, as I pressed my favorite button. No beeps for me. Yet.

Ten minutes between calls was a lovely luxury, especially on a Sunday morning. I didn't understand why the collections department was even opened on Sundays. It's not as if a payment was going to process today. Corporate America is a bitch. "So…" Ahmad grinned and tossed the ball at me. I caught it and tossed it right back. "What you do last night?"

"Went to the club?"

He shrugged and tossed the ball back a little harder. "You find yourself a new boo?"

I chunked the ball at him. "I don't go out looking for men."

"Who gon' buy your drinks?"

"Me."

"Girl, you better find you a sugar daddy to take care of you. I always keep me a lil something on the side." Smiling, he threw the ball again.

"Damn shame," I muttered, stopping in mid-sentence when the Puerto Rican princess came running down the aisle between us.

"What time is it?" she gasped, throwing her purse down on her desk that's adjacently across the aisle from me, sitting directly in front of Ahmad. So, he not only got a view of the back of my pretty hair, but hers, too.

"Good morning to you, too, Chanel," I purred and tossed the ball to Ahmad. "Nine after," I told her. She was already logging in her phone and shuffling her stack of scrap paper around, silencing her cell phone and turning on her computer, trying to find a place to set down her coffee between all her pictures and fake flowers and the multitude of testosterone-killing shit that is eating her workspace. How she lived with that kind of clutter for forty hours a week was a mystery to me.

She turned around and looked at Ahmad. "Did you hear about that shooting last night at Coyote Ugly?"

"Yeah, but nobody got hurt."

She exhaled a sigh of relief.

"What's got you all in a tizzy?" I asked Chanel.

"Nothing, thank you," she said sharply over her shoulder.

I held up my hands and made a mockingly apologetic face at Ahmad that made him snort, and pitched him the ball.

"Chanel, I'm going to grab some coffee. You want me to put something away for you?" Ahmad asked her.

She swung around in her chair. Her face lit up as if he had just offered her a million bucks. "Thanks, Ahmad." She smiled at him while handing him her packed lunch, which was probably her standard Marie Callender's frozen meal.

"No problem, anything for you." He smiled at her.

"I would like a muffin. Thanks for asking, Ahmad," I taunted. Chanel, with her evil self, whipped around and glared at me.

"Do you mind not yelling? There are people on the phone, Desiree, and even if they don't mind, I do," Chanel nastily blurted

"My bad," I replied, turning up my nose, as she rolled her eyes at me. It's not as if Chanel and I are exactly bosom buddies, but Jesus Christ, the girl needed sex, and bad.

"Look, I'm—" Chanel started, but didn't get much farther when my voice cut her off.

"Good morning, this is Desiree, how many I help you?" I smiled at Chanel when I answered a call, and I turned toward my computer. "Let me get you to the proper department, hold please." When I ended the call, I turned back to the aisle as Ahmad slowly walked up with a cup in hand.

"Where's my muffin?"

"I ate it." He laughed.

"Desiree." Chanel sighed at me and I arched an eyebrow at her. "I'm sorry I snapped like that, I just," she started before taking a call. "Good morning, this is Chanel. How may I help you?"

I glanced at Ahmad.

"Did she just apologize to you?" he mouthed.

I nodded with a shrug, and mouthed, "Yes."

"Uh-huh, no, I…Yes, I do understand…" came from Chanel, talking to whomever was on the other end of her phone line, and I tuned it out. Then came, "Excuse me?" Chanel gasped. "Sir, I am not…hello? Sir?" She looked down at her phone and confirmed the line was disconnected, and yep, the customer had hung up on her. No one said anything for a minute, and Chanel was sitting very still, but it didn't hide the way her hands were shaking. I looked a little closer. I swallowed and my eyes got big when I noticed her eyes were also watering. Damn, she didn't need to start her day this way, not when she had nine more hours ahead of her, and she was already late.

"Chanel, girl you, all right?" Ahmad gently asked, knocking Chanel out of her deep thoughts.

I leaned away from her, even though there was a good two feet between us across the aisle.

"Fuck this," she yelled, throwing her headset on her desk, jumping to her feet and stomping down the aisle toward the break room.

Ahmad and I looked at each other, wondering what was going on.

I tilted my head for Ahmad to go after her.

"I can't, man, my break's over. I gotta get back in," Ahmad said, pointing at the phone, flashing red with calls holding, putting his headset back on. I flipped him the bird as he hit his Auto-In button, turning toward his computer. "Good morning, this is Ahmad..."

"Damn," I said as I checked my time. *Yeah, this girl is about to burn up my whole morning break. And I've been here for all of thirty minutes. Awesome. Employee of the year, right here, baby.* "You owe me," I hissed at him and tossed down my headset, rolling my neck.

I stand up and head toward the break room, where I could definitely hear the sounds of Chanel softly crying and, eventually, finding her yelling at someone on her cellphone. In the break room, she was sitting in a chair with her five-inch heels kicked off and her left foot curled under her skinny jeans and her shoulders shaking as her hand covered her face.

I walked over to the vending machine to get a blueberry muffin. Neither of us said anything to each other, but she looked up and rolled her eyes at me.

"I know you fucked her?" I heard her say before I walked out the break room.

Yeah, so that sucked! Now we would have to suffer all day because Chanel was mad at someone for cheating. I hurried to my seat when I saw Kelly out of her office and on the floor. I mouthed to Ahmad "Drama" as I pushed the Auto-In button. A few seconds later, my Instant Messenger was blinking. I assumed it was Ahmad because we always communicated with Instant Messenger when we didn't want anyone to know what we were discussing. But to my surprise, it wasn't Ahmad.

10:36 AM Roland Dumas: Good morning

10:37 AM Desiree Bryant: good morning

10:37 AM Roland Dumas: How are you today? By the way, you look nice today.

10:50 AM Desiree Bryant: I'm good, and thanks. What are you doing, watching me? LOL

10:5 7 AM Roland Dumas: It's a nice sight, why wouldn't I look? The key to it all is paying attention to the little things. Wink Wink

10:57 AM Desiree Bryant: lol, well thanks. What do you want from me? LOL

10:57 AM Roland Dumas: Not sure truthfully, at the moment trying to figure out where your head is and where you're headed, but I will allow your imagination to fill in the blanks.

10:58 AM Desiree Bryant: My mind is in the gutter right now LOL. So are you looking to be my service man?

10:59 AM Roland Dumas: Is this a job interview? Are you hiring? Just kidding. I'm overly cautious with people I deal with. They don't make women like they used to and with the reality show, social media age, it's crazy

10:59 AM Desiree Bryant: sounds like you're picking the wrong women

10:59 AM Roland Dumas: LOL No I don't. Women sign up with a mutual understanding and then they try to revise their predetermined verbal contract and once their needs are not agreed to they want to blast on social media

11:00 AM Desiree Bryant: sounds like you have a lot of drama

11:01 AM Roland Dumas: This hasn't happened to me personally, but I have witnessed it. I'm modest and don't like attention. I'm more of a behind the scene stealth moving type.

11:02 AM Roland Dumas: Women make it easy these days, not all but most

11:03 AM Desiree Bryant: Well I love and value my mind, body and soul. I'm self-confident and I know I want a committed relationship and I will not settle for less than I deserve. But I do know that every man is not out to play games. There are still good men out there who would love to experience my talents. Selfless.

11:10 AM Roland Dumas: Deep. Yet simple and understandable. Well I'm selfish so I'm focused on me.

Hahahaha. What constitutes games? Is a mutual under-standing between two adults a game?

11:20 AM Desiree Bryant: I've been told I don't pick up on signs that someone is interested and I feel like if a guy is interested I shouldn't have to guess or watch for clues. Too many people want to be single and in a relationship at the same time.

11:21 AM Roland Dumas: I agree with both. If we want you, you will know. Guys are not verbal that often.

11:22 AM Roland Dumas: What talents are you speaking on?

11:22 AM Desiree Bryant: Sex

Roland was one of the facilitators during my four-week training. He was definitely not hard on the eyes at all at six-foot-three. He wore a Caesar haircut, dark complexion with light brown eyes. He played basketball, so he was in amazing shape. He had that bad boy, arrogant attitude he used on all the girls, but then that sweet boy next-door charm he used when he wanted something. Let the Rumor Mill tell it, a lot of the women around here lusted after him as if he were the only man who worked here.

Roland flirted with me during training, but nothing that too noticeable or anything to speak about. It started with general conversation like "What are your plans for the evening?" or "How was your weekend?" progressing to "Who did you spend your evening and weekend with?" along with flirtatious talk about my outfits, a wink, smile, touching of my hair and brushing himself against to me.

11:24 AM Roland Dumas: I've heard you and Veronica talking. So, I've heard about your wet snapper, not to mention the infamous leg lock that has guys skeeting on the drop of a dime, and I can only imagine that the inside of your mouth feels warm and moist like a cake baked from scratch. Need I continue?

11:25 AM Desiree Bryant: Hilarious. So, you were listening, I see. Men can't just look at me and say "hey she has skills." LOL

11:25 AM Roland Dumas: The devil is a liar. All they have to do is pay attention

11:26 AM Desiree Bryant: You're funny. I don't walk around broadcasting

11:28 AM Roland Dumas: You don't have to, men can often tell by the way you carry yourself, your walk, the contours of your mouth, the gap between your thighs from behind and how you cross your legs. There are some women who have the tools and don't know what to do with it. Body crazy and no moves or rhythm, mouth as pretty as freshly printed money and have no skills whatsoever.

11:30 AM Desiree Bryant: LMBO. Well they treat me as the good friend who they talk about their whores to.

11:35 AM Roland Dumas: They're trying to feel you out, wonder what's behind the scenes, classic lady in the streets, freak in the sheets. They may feel you will take too much work and it's hard to put in work when females are damn near giving it away like government cheese.

11:40 AM Desiree Bryant: Well I refuse to lower my standards

11:41 AM Roland Dumas: Most insecure men don't like challenges. Nowadays guys don't wanna wait a week and often don't have to.

11:50 AM Roland Dumas: Enough of that, when are you going to let me take you out?

11:53 AM Desiree Bryant: you don't waste any time I see

11:53 AM Roland Dumas: there is no need to, when I see something I like I go for it

11:54 AM Desiree Bryant: so you like something over here

11:54 AM Roland Dumas: Most definitely and I know I would love to put a smile on your face. My directness often works in my favor. LOL

11:55 AM Desiree Bryant: I already wear a lovely smile everyday….lol

11:56 AM Roland Dumas: I can put a REAL smile on your face

11:58 AM Desiree Bryant: Oh I see. Well that would be nice, so how do you plan on doing that?

11:59 AM Roland Dumas: If you let me take you out you can find out. Here is my number text me so I can lock your number in my phone. 757-555-2137

11:59 AM Desiree Bryant: Ok. Don't make me regret this

The volumes of calls were slow, so I spent the rest of my day reading magazines, talking to Ahmad and messaging Roland. What a long day. I truly hated working on Sundays. Hated it.

"A'ight, I'm out," I said, turning off my computer monitor and logging out of my phone. Seven P.M. on the dot and not a moment too soon.

"Sure you don't want to reconsider?" Ahmad asked after shutting down his computer and winding up his headset cord. I swivel my chair to face him. "It will be fun, drinks are half price on Sundays," he said, trying to convince me again to go to the bar after I declined his offer earlier today.

I chuckled and shook my head. "I'll pass. I'm tired and I need rest, so I can make it here on time tomorrow." Ahmad laughed. "I may hit you up later though," I added.

"And on that note," Ahmad said quickly, standing and leaning forward, his voice soft when he whispered, "Night, Chanel," who was stuck on a call that sounded like it was nowhere near being finished.

"Uh-huh, no…absolutely," she said into her headset and then muted my phone. "Night, Ahmad." She smiled at him then unmuted the call. "That must have been terrible, I'm so sorry…"

I gave Ahmad a two-finger salute in a sendoff, as he headed down the aisle toward the stairway. I looked at my cell phone. No text messages meant no drama, which I could definitely use.

"Uh-huh, so how many payments would you like to set up?" Chanel muted her phone and glanced at me. "I am never getting out of here."

I looked around the empty floor, as most people already cleared out. I put my phone in my pocket and smiled at the janitor, who was coming down the aisle to empty the trashcans, looking smelly with unkempt cornrows.

"Hello," I mumbled, as he tilts his head toward Chanel.

"What's up?" he asked, looking directly at my breast. "You leaving?" Now he was looking at me from the corner of his eye.

"Yup, I'm out of here."

"Take your time." He grinned, looking at me as if we were best buddies and had been forever.

Creep.

I handed him my trash can, he emptied it, changed the bag, and handed it back to me. After replacing the trash can under my desk, I looked over at Chanel, and caught Mr. Ragamuffin bending down, grabbing the trashcan underneath Chanel's desk, and rubbing her thigh. He gathered the bag and replaced it with a fresh one, while looking at Chanel as if she were his playmate. Something about him just didn't sit right with me.

"Have a good night, sweetheart," he said, nodding at me and continuing down the aisle. I didn't respond, but my glare followed him until I turned to walk away.

"Goodnight, Chanel," I said loudly, her eyes widened as she shooed me away with her hand.

"No, sorry about that. Please, you're fine, we're in no hurry. Uh-huh, no it's okay, I promise…" I heard Chanel sweetly saying, trying to appease the caller as I headed down the aisle, swinging my keys around my finger.

As I got closer to the elevator, I heard familiar voices whispering in an empty office. I stopped at the cracked door and eavesdropped. I overheard Kelly and Michelle, both managers, talking about someone in the department.

"I don't know why she's trying to be our friend. It's not like she's going to get promoted or move up in the company. There aren't any management positions available and I'm not going to befriend her, so she can stab me in the back and take my job." Kelly's manly-looking ass said defensively.

"You know how some people are, they think if they kiss your ass it will get them far," Michelle added

Kelly cleared her throat. "Going forward, don't put her on any special projects and don't allow her to run any meetings. She will sit in her seat and take calls. I will not allow her to step on my toes and take my job, but I need you to support me on this because she can take your job, too."

I ran off and onto the elevator. I hurried to my car, thinking I should have taken Ahmad up on his offer to go out for drinks because this place was a goddamn circus.

CHAPTER THREE

Roland

At exactly 10:25 a.m., I walked into the conference room and slid into a chair next to Cynthia, ready for the ten-thirty meeting. I realized all the agents from the outbound collections team were there. Sheldon and Tsuki were seated at the far end of the table, looking over a packet of papers. Ronald, who walked in a few minutes after Lynette, sat across from her, doodling nervously on a pad of paper. Derrick and Cynthia spoke quietly to each other about *American Horror Story* that was on television the previous night.

I sat at the table, daydreaming about last night's sex festival with Trina from Customer Service. Cynthia tapped my hand, bringing my attention back to the front of the room as Clarence and Michelle walked in the door and took their seats at the head of the table.

"I guess you're wondering why we called you all here today," said Michelle. "Before I start, I need your assurance that what we tell you this morning will not leave this room. Is everyone clear on that?"

All heads nodded.

"I won't sugarcoat this," Clarence chimed in. "If I find out that any of this information leaks, I'll have your job. Immediately. No exceptions." He looked at each person. "Got it?"

I nodded, anticipating the bombshell that was about to dropped on us.

"Here's the deal, people," Clarence started. "We've learned that we may be going through an acquisition." There were a few gasps around the table. "We've been approached by several buyers as the possible purchase." Majority of the people simply stared at Clarence, completely dumbfounded by the information he just dropped on us.

I spoke up. "When did this happen, Clarence?"

"A few months ago the rumors started, but I didn't think anything would come of it." Suddenly, the room erupted in a ball of questions.

"What will happen to my job?" Sheldon asked.

"Who will my boss be?" Derrick followed up without allowing Sheldon's question to be answered.

"I just need to know: will I have to move?" Ronald confusingly added, not talking to anyone in particular.

"So what's the plan?" Cynthia asked, taking interest in the conversation for the first time since the start of the meeting.

I wanted to protest all these ridiculous questions, but I didn't want to make a scene. But, I made no effort to hide my agitation of the foolishness.

"For now, we're going to continue with business as usual," Michelle said, looking at Clarence. "Anything else, Clarence?"

The room fell silent, except for the ticking of a large clock hanging on the wall. Everyone jumped at the sound of Beyoncé's voice singing the remake of her song "Crazy in Love" from the movie *Fifty Shades of Grey* coming from inside Lynette's purse.

"I'm so sorry," Lynette embarrassingly said.

A few people giggled then the room fell silent again from all the side conversations, as Clarence's voice spoke up. "If you get approached by anyone from the media, by phone or outside the building, notify both Michelle and myself immediately. We'll try to do damage control, if needed." Clarence stood, effectively ending the meeting. He and Michelle left, and everyone else slowly filed out behind them—some shocked and extremely upset.

I walked back to my desk and settled in my chair, preparing to start my shift. I opened my email—twenty new messages from the female fan club, an email about some policy changes, and a bunch of junk mail. I nearly jumped when I heard a voice behind me.

My eyes widened. "Roland. What's going on, buddy?" Glen said, with a smile.

I closed Outlook, but I didn't really know how long he had been standing there, looking over my shoulder. For all I know, he could have scanned all my emails.

I returned the smile, smiling for the first time since leaving the meeting. "Same ol' same ol'. Did you catch the game last night?" I asked.

Glen rubbed his hands together. "Of course, NBA is where it's at?" He laughed. A few seconds later, Sheldon made his way over to my cubicle. "I'll talk with you later, Roland. How you doing, Sheldon?" Glen said, as he walked away.

"Great!" Sheldon replied, patting Glen on the back.

"Good timing, Bro. I couldn't figure out how to get rid of him," I jokingly said.

Sheldon looked over his shoulder. "Wow! Do you really think this is going to happen?"

"Who knows with this place," I replied.

My phone began to vibrate, alerting I'd received a text message.

"Hey. Just saw your message. We still on for later? 9 pm."

I looked at the message for a moment, running through the list of people I know who might be texting me this early in the morning, considering I didn't recognize the number. Did I make plans with someone without knowing?

"Who is this?" I texted, waiting for a response that came moments later.

"Who do you think it is? You forgot about me already?"

What the fuck? My facial expression mirrored my thoughts—blank. I had not a clue. It was obviously a wrong number.

"Seriously! Who is this?" I hit send, but this time a reply didn't come right away, so I continued reading my emails. A few minutes later, my phone vibrated.

"Look up. We've been watching you. Your face has been priceless."

I laughed out loud when I looked up to see Veronica and Desiree waving in my direction. I texted back, "Tell Desiree since she wants to play games then she has to fulfill that invitation so I expect to see her at 9 sharp." I put my phone away, got out of my chair, and walked toward the training room.

"Hey, Boo."

I turned my head in the direction of the voice, coming across my favorite shorthaired red head. "Toni, hey love." I smiled, hugging her.

She mischievously smiled and slowly slid her hand up my arm. "How have you been doing without me?"

I returned her suggestive smile with a devious grin, since I already knew where this was going.

"I've been so sad without you," I replied coolly, playing along with her game. "You know how I am when I'm being ignored…"

"I didn't mean to," she said in a fake, teary tone. "I was just giving you the space that you were asking for, so I found someone else to temporarily have fun with…"

Softly laughing, I started eyeing her toned, long legs, overpowering the short skirt she was wearing. My memory flashed back—Toni loved sucking dick, licking nuts like a lollipop and swallowing.

"Having fun without me?" I teased back.

Toni caressed my cheek then my chin, then, holding my face as if it were fragile.

I cleared my throat, adjusting my hard on, trying to think of anything, anything to clear my fucking head and stop thinking about all the nasty shit Toni and I did.

"But, I'll never have as much fun as I have with you," she replied, as she pursed her luscious lips. "I'm all yours."

From the outside, I remained cool and calm with an expressionless face. But inside, I was grinning. I'd already reeled her in. By saying those words, I knew that I could dispose on her whenever I wanted.

It was all too easy. Sure, she had a pretty face with a curvaceous body, but so did almost every other female at this job. My name had been thrown into someone's conversation at least ten times a day. I wanted a challenge, something hard. Someone that was hard to get. At least until I'd managed to reel her in. I wanted someone other than this beautiful, insecure female that was standing right beside me.

From the corner of my eye, I noticed Joy walking toward my direction. She was like a sister to me, so she knew a lot of my secrets. "Hey, bruh." She playfully tapped my shoulder and smiled.

"What's up, sis?" I replied, as she passed by.

I returned my attention to Toni after she wrapped her right pinky around mine. "Call me sometimes. I miss you."

I nodded, acknowledging I had heard what she said and walked off toward the training room.

I was logged into my instant messenger and I saw that Kemi was online, too. I've been trying to date her for a while. Usually, whenever I sent her a chat message, she would respond instantly and we would talk about whatever was on her mind. But lately, she's been standoffish.

12:35 PM Roland Dumas: Good afternoon Ol' lady how are ya? I was trying to talk to you earlier but I guess you didn't hear me.

12:35 PM Kemi Townsley: Not sure what you're referring to but I'm good.

12:36 PM Roland Dumas: Nothing in particular, I was just saying I was trying to speak and you kept walking.

12:37 PM Kemi Townsley: OOOOO

12:39 PM Roland Dumas: That's what I'm waiting to hear either whispered softly in my ear or echoing off the walls while being enticed from behind.

12:40 PM Kemi Townsley: Huh?

12:40 PM Roland Dumas: No hidden meaning. Direct comment. I miss you.

12:41 PM Kemi Townsley: You miss lil ol' me? LOL Really? Why so?

12:43 PM Roland Dumas: It's something about you. I have baby-stepped my way around the globe dealing with you. LOL

12:45 PM Kemi Townsley: I'm really into church and I'm in a relationship with Jesus Christ right now. I no longer drink, smoke or party. I'm not having sex anymore. I'm celibate. You didn't do anything wrong. I need to become re-centered and refocused. Sorry if you feel I wasted your time but we are on two different paths.

12:50 PM Roland Dumas: I see you're making changes with your life and that's cool you will never know or grow if you don't take chances and you haven't even given me a chance. I can show you better than I can tell you.

12:51 PM Roland Dumas: I'm not just looking for sex. I want a real woman in my life; you didn't even ask me what I'm looking for or what my goals are. I would like to make changes to my life as well. But I'm sure it will all work out for ya.

12:55 PM Kemi Townsley: You're being very open, honest, forthcoming and emotional today. Interesting...

12:58 PM Roland Dumas: LMBO I'm always honest... now that emotional part I disagree. R. Kelly and Jay-Z made a song about the power of the pussy. But nobody has to tell you about that because you're walking around with that leaky snapper. Lord knows I miss that as well as that outlandish amount of cheat meat aka breast.

12:59 PM Roland Dumas: So you pretty much used me to get you right and reset your clock. No harm no foul. Respect due.

1:00 PM Roland Dumas: Men will try even though you said what you said. No means no but doesn't mean stop trying randomly.

1:05 PM Kemi Townsley: Wow you are scaring me; you are coming off way too strong. It's nothing against you or your past I'm just not interested in pursuing a friendship or relationship at all.

1:08 PM Roland Dumas: I was just messing with you; you're sounding like a totally new woman.

1:12 PM Kemi Townsley: I'm working.

For a moment, I contemplated over how I should respond, but without another thought, I left it alone. Her stuck up ass can keep that holier than thou shit over there because she was sexting me two weeks ago. My eyes shifted to my phone as the screen lit up, letting me know I had a text message. I signed in and picked up my phone, tapping the screen to enter my pass code and looking at the text. I leaned back in the chair as I read the text, a small smile coming to my lips.

It was Trina.

"Meet up, tonight?"

Before I had time to formulate a response, I received a lengthy text from her going in about her feelings toward me, blah, blah, blah. I frowned slightly; I didn't like lengthy text messages. Those who texted me knew it was a pet peeve of mine. I'm more of a one-word reply type of guy.

It had been at least a week since I had sex and I was getting sexually frustrated, so I replied with *"Yes."*

"You sure are popular," Melissa, my cubical mate, said as she strolled beside me, glimpsing curiously at my phone. I had a special place in my heart for older women and Melissa, in her own way, reminded me of my grandmother. Disregarding all the other mushy emotional stuff Trina was talking about, I quickly put my phone back in my pocket.

"Yeah, I guess, Ms. Melissa." I laughed a little, as her probing light brown eyes peered at me.

There was silence, which I believe was because Ms. Melissa was drinking her coffee, but then she muttered out, "Ladies man." She giggled; her voice was so soft, as soft as the snow outside.

I turned around and grinned from ear to ear. "Stop starting stuff, I'm just enjoying life, Ms. Melissa. I have no intentions of getting married right now, even though I do plan to eventually marry and have a family, but no time soon."

CHAPTER FOUR

Chanel

Ever heard the expression: *Life's a bitch, and then you die?* At thirty-seven, death seemed close because this bitch wouldn't leave me alone. My life's story...was a complicated one. It was one where you take pity on the one who lived through it. Fuck pity; I didn't need anyone's pity and I was not going to take it. My past does not define me, but right now, it was playing a major role in the present.

I grew up in Puerto Rico and lost my accent once I was shipped here to Virginia at eleven years old. Being exposed to the English language on a daily basis my Aunt Sofia allowed me to be bilingual, which caused my accent to fade. The only time it was prevalent was when I attempted to form an English sentence.

The day my parents sent me away will always remain etched in psyche. My mami and I were dancing in our kitchen, listening to Celia Cruz's "Ritmo en el Corazon" flowing from the speakers of the radio. My papi came in and danced with us and we all laughed because he had no rhythm, but it never stopped him from shaking and moving.

"Chanel," Papi said, kneeling down, placing his hand on my shoulder. "My beautiful baby girl, listen closely, okay?" I nodded and glanced at mi madre *(my mother)*, who was behind him speaking quietly on the phone. "Your mami and I love you more than anything in this world. We know you're going to grow up to be a beautiful, intelligent woman and you will make us proud, but we have to send you to Virginia to live with your aunt and uncle. Right now, mija *(my daughter)*, we're going through some hard times." As he spoke, he reached into his pocket, pulled out a locket, and placed it around my neck. "Whenever you're scared or need your mami and papi, you look at this and keep it close to your heart. Your mami and I will always be with you, mija." He then kissed my head as my mami rushed over to me and pulled me into a bone-crushing hug and kissed my cheek.

"We love you, mija," she said.

I couldn't utter a word. The burning sensation of tears welled up and finally fell. I just hugged them both as my tears continued to cascade. We were living in very poor conditions, but I didn't understand why my parents would send me thousands of miles away to have someone else raise me.

It was my junior year in high school when I started going off the deep end and my "slut status" began. My promiscuity knew no gender, as it followed me into college. I was stupid enough to think I could leave that shit behind once I left home for college, but I didn't. I realized my wants and needs changed, but my actions didn't. There was no one to talk to about the issues brewing inside me. My parents lived in Puerto Rico and I never trusted anyone else, so I started drinking.

At first, it was every other day, then every day, then three or four times a day. I found myself reaching for a drink even when I was thirsty for water. Then, I met Elvin my senior year of college. He was a great person, smart, funny and even a romantic. I had never been exposed to a man with these qualities, and I knew if anything was to become of our relationship, this had to change. I couldn't even remember what laughing felt like before Elvin. My cheek and mouth muscles were in constant pain from laughter. I knew that soon I would have to let him in on who I really was. At this point, I was already neck deep in my constant drinking.

Elvin kept me so busy with dates, cuddling and even phone conversations that Captain Morgan must have begun to get jealous. I was completely functional, so it wasn't until three months in to our relationship when he noticed. I'll never forget how the sun warmly caressed my face the morning Papi called me to say Maria, a childhood friend, had been murdered in San Juan. My heart sank and tears dropped as soon as the phone hit the sidewalk. For days, I stayed away from Elvin—no calls, texts, nada. I decided to silence my phone so everything was screened. Three days later, as I lay on my couch, with vodka in hand, my front door swung open, followed by a breeze and a six-foot-two-inch frame. Elvin came for me as our eyes met, his gaze just told me how hurt, sad and disappointed he was to see me in this disheveled state. Stained tee, ripped panties, the stench of alcohol and musk. I know he had no idea who lay in front of him.

He wasn't happy nor was he okay with it. He made it very clear he couldn't be in a relationship with an alcoholic. That was the first time anyone called me an alcoholic to my face. I was head over heels in love with him after a few months of dating, so I was willing to do anything to keep him. I decided to get my shit together and four months later, he became my fiancé. Of course, I wasn't ready to give up drinking; I just got a little better at hiding it by using mouthwash, strong perfumes, and plenty of gum.

To this day, I struggled with anger, lack of attention, social and depression problems that stemmed from my childhood. With my anger issues, I was shocked this job lasted as long as it had—ten years. Within that time, Elvin and I had gotten married, had two beautiful children, and got divorced. He did his best to keep me away from my liquid vice, but he would always come out on the losing end. Seven years in, and that was his final straw. I'm now a single mother of two: six-year-old Camila and a four-year-old Jeremy. Although Elvin couldn't be with me, he remained a prominent and valid figure in his children's lives.

Today at work, I felt like the walking dead. I was broken from my trance when Ahmad tugged on my arm, letting me know it was lunchtime.

"They're hiring extremely too many people, there's no place to park in the morning and this café is like a zoo, animals running around everywhere," Ahmad said, as we sat down in the booth.

"Half of these people won't even make it to their ninety-day mark," I said, munching on a French fry. "So, place your bet. What's the percentage of new hires do you think will be here an entire year? The winner will get free lunch at the local spot of their choice."

Ahmad took a small bite of his burger and slowly chewed. "Girl, how you gon' ask me that when I didn't think I would be here a week? Let's say 45%," he answered in his usual deep voice. "But I don't think that many of the tenured reps will be here either," he added with a raised eyebrow and devilish smirk.

"Did you just see that shit?" I asked changing the subject while staring, as a female walked past with green, red, blue, and yellow hair.

"Girl, don't start acting all phony like you're shocked to see her hair like that." Ahmad twisted his lips before laughing. "The way these girls dress in this here workplace is way beyond inappropriate, looking like they're going to the club or chilling on the couch on a Saturday morning, stinking up the place.

Loud hooting and rowdy laughter from a nearby table took my attention off that craziness with the hair. Trina from Customer Service was at the next table running her mouth, probably about nothing and the entire table was laughing. Trina and I made eye contact, so I forced a fake smile before rolling my eyes. I never really cared much for Trina because her name was always the eye of any drama hurricane that hit this place.

"Anyway, did you hear about the two females in the training class that started shouting and then started fighting? Messing up makeup all over a seat. I heard Roland took one of the females, Lisa, out the room and while they were walking through the doorway, Shavelle, the other girl, ran up and swung on Lisa from behind, almost hitting Roland in the back of the head."

Ahmad was filling my head with so much craziness, I covered my mouth with my hands in an attempt to stop myself from screaming. I was happy to be hearing about someone else's foolishness rather than dealing with my own reality.

Laughing hysterically, Ahmad continued to speak. "Girl! Hair, shoes, and papers were flying. Jim the trainer got tangled up when they started punching and pushing. Needless to say, they both were terminated that very moment."

I leaned forward in my seat. "How do you find out all this stuff?"

"You know I know people all over this building that keeps the tea!" Ahmad replied while clasping his arms behind his head.

"Wait! You heard about Cynthia that works in Customer Service? Honey, she was swiftly walked out for stealing credit card numbers?"

"Isn't that Lynette's friend?" Ahmad questioned with a raised brow.

"Yup, I think they started in training together." I nodded in agreeance.

"That's messed up. I wonder what she was buying. I hope Gucci, Tom Ford and cash advances to cover her living expenses because I don't think she's going to get unemployment," Ahmad said. We couldn't help but burst out in laughter.

I looked up and was now making eye contact with another person I disliked, Veronica. I eyed her for a second walking into the café as I continued to speak. I heard she got caught because she used the credit card number to purchase plane tickets for herself, her kids, and husband.

"What's up with that?" Ahmad inquired.

"I just told you, she used the card to purchase airline tickets."

"No, not that. What's up with you, Veronica and Desiree? What the hell are those devil stares for?"

"I don't have beef with them, I just don't like Veronica. She's phony and thinks her shit don't stink, walking around with a fifty-inch weave in her hair. Veronica and I used to hang out all the time, pretty much every weekend. We even went down to Mardi Gras together. We were so drunk one night that we were crawling in the streets all the way back to the hotel." To my surprise, I giggled at the memory. "I even allowed her ungrateful ass to sleep on my couch for a few weeks when she was between places."

"Oh, that's my type of party Mardi Gras," Ahmad returned the laughter

"Desiree is just annoying and dumb, idiot is sleeping with Roland, and so is everyone else. Quiet as it's kept, Veronica fucked Roland back in the day on the low and now Desiree, her own cousin, is getting that. Veronica is trifling; I just don't trust that chick."

"Well you're sleeping with the janitor," Ahmad slid in nonchalantly while he took a sip of his Lipton lemonade tea.

I gasped; my mouth flew open and could have hit the table along with Ahmad's words. That was supposed to be a secret.

I began stuttering. "I can't believe you just said that. How do you know?"

"Honey, I see and hear ev-e-ry-*thang*....nothing gets past me. Plus I saw you sneaking out of the janitor closet one day last month. So if your sneaky ass is going to be fucking at work make sure you cover your tracks and I'm not talking about weave. I could almost smell the sex from down the hall." Ahmad said condescendingly.

"Awk-warrrd." I was so embarrassed I wanted to cry and I'm sure my face was beet red, so I just smiled and didn't say anything for a few seconds. If Ahmad knew about Jermaine and me then no telling whom else knew. I looked Ahmad in the eye and quickly changed the subject, but before I could speak, Roland walked up.

"I heard you had to be a referee for a boxing match?" I slightly giggled.

"That was crazy. It doesn't surprise me though; things have truly changed since I started here. I will continue to do my job until I decide to leave or they ask me to leave," Roland said, wearing a look of pure disgust. "I have to go. Y'all have a good one," he added before walking away.

Once Roland walked away, Ahmad looked at me as if to say *back to the real topic at hand, Jermaine.* I stared at Ahmad. I needed to know I could trust him before I revealed my secret and disclosed all the juicy details about Jermaine and me. Ahmad had to be one of the realest, down to earth comedians I've ever met. I've always thought of gay men to be slightly messy though. Ahmad has always had my back though and never faltered.

CHAPTER FIVE

Kelly

I flew down the hallway in complete panic. What I saw on my computer resulted in wings on my feet and a massive lump in my throat. *What the hell is going on?* I thought, as I finally reached the conference room. Opening the door, I hesitated for a moment before gathering the courage to enter.

Three pairs of eyes turned toward me as they waited for our weekly management meeting. Clarence, Michelle, and Pam gave me questioning looks, as I tried to catch my breath from the panic attack that was forming inside me. I could tell by their expressions that none of them knew what had happened, yet; I didn't know if this was a good thing or not. It meant I would have to be the bearer of the terrible news, which was a role that definitely did not suit me well. Before I had recovered my ability to speak, to explain what was going on, Glen walked into the room. I could tell instantly by his stiff composure and the thunderous look on his face that he definitely had spoken with

Human Resources. "Oh God," I whispered, as Glen turned his dark eyes on me.

"Kelly?" Glen uttered my name as a question, but the expression on his face was so grim and foreboding, no other words were necessary. I swallowed, knowing myself and others in the room were in serious trouble.

"What exactly happened?" Glen, his voice even, emotionlessly stared at each one of his managers in turn; everyone was totally clueless as to what was happening.

"Glen, I know it looks bad, really bad." My face got redder as I spoke. Glen stared at me in silence.. Clarence looked at me with his eyebrows raised in question. "Last week, when we stayed the extra night in Tampa." I threw appealing glances at the others. I knew Glen would soon be tearing strips off our backs for the heat we brought on us. It seemed funny at the time, as most things do when the participants are drunk, but in the cold light of day, we all broke the code of ethics. "Well, Glen, you probably remember that we all decided to go for a drink, to relax after that long boring meeting." I, once again, looked at the others, hoping someone would help me out, but again, they all held their silence. Turning back to Glen I continued. "And then, after you and Clarence left, we, uh, we decided to play a drinking game…" My voice trailed off, as I saw the expression on Glen's face. I opened and closed my mouth a couple of times, but paralysis of regret grabbed hold of my vocal cords, so I said nothing.

"Would someone like to tell me what's going on here?" Clarence questioned.

My voice free of its stronghold, I averted my eyes from Glen's extremely angry eyes, and I spoke in a voice that was barely above a whisper. "I think this has gotten out of hand." I swallowed hard, tears of shame starting to run down my cheeks.

"What's going on?" Clarence questioned again, his voice slightly angry.

"Well, Clarence, it seems this trio of managers spent the evening getting *drunk*." Glen's voice rose, emphasizing the word drunk, causing Michelle and Pam, to shrink a little in their seats. "Then, it appears, they had the wonderful idea to discuss work gossip in a bar full of people, including employees of the company from our Tampa site."

I had an extremely bad feeling about where this was going, and looked at the others in embarrassment.

Michelle finally spoke up. "Glen, we were just letting our hair down and having fun. We didn't know anyone in there worked for the company and we definitely didn't think anyone would hear us talking, no harm no foul." Michelle's optimism seeped out of her voice as she glanced between Glen and me, probably feeling like a huge boulder lifted off her chest, as she exhaled deeply.

Pam, deciding she should speak up, as I was still mute, spoke up next. "We were joking, Glen. We all drank too much; spoke a little too freely about certain subjects."

"Yes, we did it. We were all drunk. We didn't do it with malice," Michelle spoke up, anger oozing off her voice. Turning toward Pam, she continued. "We had spent the evening talking about our sexual adventures when we were younger, then we talked about work and, yes, we said some inappropriate things." Even as Michelle gave a brief description to Glen in a flat, emotionless voice, I felt my heart squeeze with shame and regret. Michelle was covering her eyes, assumingly trying to stem the embarrassment that had surfaced. Michelle started to speak again, but one look at Glen and she immediately recoiled, her face turning tomato red.

I decided I might as well continue and put it all out there on the table. I knew this had to be serious if Human Resources was now involved. "We were joking around, acting like commentaries—"My voice suddenly cut off as I vaguely remembered some of the things we had said. My eyes welled as I remembered everything word—talking while drunk. I blinked, and continued. "But it was just us joking around. We weren't looking to harm anyone." I tried to stifle a sob as all eyes turned on me. I stopped to wipe the lonely tear from cheek.

Glen took a moment and then raised his eyebrows at me, with a slight nod, for me to continue, but I had reached my limit. My job was now on the line. I covered my face with my hands and shook my head.

"I need to know *everything* that was said," Glen said coldly. "I will not tolerate any surprises. Now that Human Resources is involved, a full investigation is going to take place."

Michelle's, Clarence's, and Pam's jaws dropped at this last revelation. They had not known about Human Resources and the open investigation. The silence in the room was oppressive, like the air was pressing against everyone's chest. Only Michelle's and Pam's sobs could be heard. I could understand why Glen looked ready to strangle all of us.

I could barely speak, as the sobs were thick in my throat at the thought of what was going to happen, but I forged through it. "This is what I can remember. I said that Ahmad is the typical gay guy, very emotional and always complaining about something and how bad I wanted him off my team or hoping he would eventually quit. I said that Sonny's cigar-stained breath was hot and foul and every time he spoke to me face-to-face, a pain ripped through my body." I took a deep breath, tugging nervously on my shirt before I continued. "Someone talked about how Sonya comes into work every day drenched in sweat and reeking of her own musty body order. I said Chanel is a bitch and I can't wait until the day I can walk her out the door and I will be celebrating with three shots of Tequila to celebrate her heritage. We even discussed the rumor of the possible acquisition." I fell silent, hoping someone else would add on, but no one said anything. If I hadn't learned anything else from Glen, I learned if you lie, the consequences would be worse.

Glen scanned each face before he sighed, as if the weight of the world was on his shoulders. "After speaking with a few individuals, they have no real proof, so it's going to come down to their word against all of yours. So, get your story straight before Human Resources comes to talk with you individually. If you want to keep your job, you better come up with a different version of that story you just told me, a PG version. I'll support you for as long as I can, but I don't want to hear about this all over this building," Glen commanded before walking about the room.

I shook my head as I stood up, making the chair squeak behind me. Everyone looked at me. "I need some air," I said, before exiting the room, ignoring the calls of my name. I rushed back to my desk to only be met with the smirking faces of Ahmad and Desiree. I reached across my desk, and grabbed my cell phone and car keys. Walking toward the staircase, I kept walking until I reached the parking lot. I unlocked the door and got in, closing and locking the door. I turned on the car for the air conditioner and plugged in my phone. I pressed play on my iTunes, not caring what song played. I gripped the steering wheel and dropped my head. "Fuck, fuck, fuck!" This was all becoming overwhelming, as I sat in the car for the next twenty minutes, trying to regain my composure. I heard a small knock on the passenger window. I turned my head and saw Michelle giving me a smile and gesturing to the door. I nodded, picked up my phone, and turned the music off. I unlocked the door and Michelle slid into the passenger seat and closed the door behind her.

"You okay?" Michelle asked.

"I'm fine, but let's not talk about me. We need to get our stories straight before Human Resources questions us. Do you think Pam will remember everything we come up with?"

Michelle looked at me, as if I had asked a dumb question. "Our jobs are on the line, she better remember."

"All right then." I glanced toward the building and remained quiet for a second before heading back inside.

I had hardly settled back at my desk before Keisha rushed in. "Kelly, I need a change. I'm sick of this team."

"What happened?" Today I was bombarded with all sorts of issues, but my thoughts were still on the earlier meeting with Glen

"This team acts like a bunch of high schoolers. Ugh! I'm so over this birthday club. Desiree, as well as myself, has to send out three and four emails to remind everyone to pay their $3 per birthday per person."

"Okay so what's the problem?"

"The problem is that the last email I sent said the ones who paid will eat and those who didn't pay will not be able to feast with us. Chanel, who never pays, was running her mouth, complaining about how we're supposed to be one team. It's so much negative energy and not worth my time to even acknowledge the foolishness. I don't have money to keep covering month after month."

"Calm down, it's going to be okay," I stammered, trying to sound as neutral as possible.

"It's crazy. We are all adults here. Trust me, I know we have a lot going on in our personal lives, but they think everything is free."

Chanel stormed into my cubicle. "You call yourself telling on me?"

Keisha's ponytail whipped around, as she cocked her head to the side. "I'm not telling on anyone. I'm stating the facts."

I heavily sighed and closed my eyes. "Chanel, please go back to your desk."

Keisha and Chanel exchanged nasty looks before Chanel stormed away.

"You see what I mean? Negative energy and foolishness!"

"Aye yai yai," was all I could say in reply. "We will discuss this in our next team meeting. Until then, let's just work with what we have."

"Okay, thanks." Keisha walked out my office.

"No problem," I replied, smiling awkwardly.

Chapter Six

Desiree

I swiped my badge and headed inside the building, earning a surprise glance or two from the receptionist as I passed because I wasn't running late. Surprised to no one, Ahmad was already here, sitting at his desk chatting quietly with Tsuki and Sheldon before logging in at ten.

It's a very relaxed environment, and I've been on friendly terms with all my coworkers until recently. A lot changed when my manager, Kelly, recognized me in an email for being a top performer. In it, she praised my work, but also sent a strong message to the staff indicating that their lack of interest was extremely disappointing. I found that contributed to their lax attitudes toward their jobs, their constant smoke breaks, and their gossipy attitudes.

Now, I feel like I have a target on my back, especially when Kelly, unknowingly or knowingly, pitted me against everyone, and I noticed a few of their actions toward me had become cold, unfriendly, and borderline catty, especially Chanel; she'd become very petty and vindictive. She's a troublemaker, liar, with a nasty attitude. A few of the women were very close, which had created an uncomfortable environment, since we all worked in the same room.

Ahmad's eyes widened when he saw me, as he leaned back in his chair, looking like he wanted to applaud. "Should we be expecting some miracles to come through here later?" Ahmad asked sarcastically.

I rolled my eyes. "Pretty sure they already made their rounds," I muttered, firing up my computer, and taking a sip of my coffee. I had time this morning to stop at Starbucks, and I'm still early.

"So, what was with last night?" he asked.

I turned to face him. "What do you mean?" I asked, taking another sip.

"Your phone butt dialed me and I heard you and someone having sex," he blurted out.

I almost choked on my coffee, sputtering a bit. "What?"

Chanel slammed her drawer closed, after putting something away. I swiped my finger across my neck in a plea for Ahmad to shut the fuck up. Chanel got up and walked toward Kelly's desk.

"First, you're supposed to be my friend," I snapped. He gulped. "And second," I said, glancing around, checking to make sure no one was in earshot. "I didn't sleep with anyone. He had his tongue on my lower lips." We both laughed

"Hey, girls! What are you two talking about?" said the voice coming up the aisle. It was my cousin, Veronica.

"Oh, Ahmad was just talking about his sex life," I said to Veronica

"Hey, at least I have a sex life!" Ahmad sarcastically said to the both of us.

"Sorry, Veronica and I are still virgins." I laughed.

"You may be the only two!" Ahmad said. "So, tell us, Veronica, are you still dating that sexy creature who works downstairs?"

"We broke up a few days before I came back from New York. I guess it just wasn't meant to last. And to answer your next question: yes, I am still a virgin." Veronica burst out laughing.

"All right, so I'm with Dave! Veronica just broke up with Thomas, but they will get back together. Desiree, it's time for you to get a boyfriend!" Ahmad said, playfully.

I rolled my eyes. "I am fine being single," I said. "Like Mary J said, *no drama*."

"I have to agree with Ahmad," Veronica chimed in. "You haven't had a boyfriend in like a year."

"Oh *no*, not you, too! I am fine being single. I just haven't found a guy I like yet," I said.

"Well, I heard Roland likes you," Veronica added. "Desi, so you're going to act like you haven't noticed the way he looks at you lately? Veronica glanced at me, smiling.

There was brief silence before I replied, "Roland Dumas?" I tried to playoff the obvious.

Clearing her throat, Veronica arched her brow. "You are so phony." We both laughed.

Roland spoke to me every single day when he walked in and he always made sure to say goodbye when he left.

"When he talks to you," Veronica continued, "and I'm around his gaze lingers on you a tab bit longer than he does anyone else I've seen."

"What do you mean?"

"I mean, he looks at you like he wants to eat you," Veronica joked, purring like a cat.

I remained silent for a few seconds, trying to absorb everything. "He is cute." I sighed.

Veronica chuckled. "Babies are cute, that man is *fine*." I laughed right along with her. "You better get that girl," Veronica sang, smiling, flipping her strawberry blonde weave over her shoulder, and walking away after noticing Kelly watching our every move.

After Veronica was out of earshot, Ahmad rolled his chair to my desk. "Just be careful, sis. I heard Roland messes with a bunch of people that work here. Old, young, short, tall, fat, skinny, smart, and dumb," Ahmad said with laughter

"Okay, I get it jerk." I laughed

"Desiree, Chanel is not that bad," Ahmad said, quickly changing the subject as he rolled his chair back to his desk.

"Really? Then how would you describe her?" I asked, turning to face him.

"I don't know...mean spirited."

"That's just a nice way of saying she is a bitch," I said playfully.

"Okay, damn! Fine. I admit she is a bitch! Happy now?"

I laughed. "Yeah!"

I didn't think this day could go any slower. Five o'clock and two hours to go, and the tension between Chanel and me were nauseating. At least no one else had seemed to notice, because the rest of the people in our row and practically the whole damn building had been consistently swinging by—Lynette was giggling with her girlfriends and Ahmad was talking about some damn music video, but I was not in the mood to join the conversation.

I was thinking another date with Roland was absolutely on my itinerary tonight. But for now, I'd continue sitting in my chair with my head leaned back, eyes closed and twirling a pen between my fingers, as I wait for a call.

"Two more hours," I said aloud.

"Desiree," The department manager, Glen, called out and my eyes flew open.

"Hey, Glen. How's it going?" I said casually, but his face was too tight and damn it, I didn't need this now.

"You got a minute?"

"Sure." I forced a smile and switched my phone status into a meeting code, setting down my headset and following him back to his office.

"So, how have you been?" he asked, as I walked into his office.

"Fine."

"Good." He nodded, his hands folded in his lap.

It annoyed the shit out of me when he acted like he was on some middle-aged, corporate, end-all-be-all, but apparently that qualified him to bullshit me around when all I wanted was to be left alone to do my damn job.

"Pulled some calls, they sounded good."

I nodded, wishing he'd get on with whatever the fuck this was actually about. I knew he didn't want to talk about my calls. They had to 'check in' once every few weeks and he had hit me up last week, so I already knew this had nothing to do with what's happening on the phone.

"So, I wanted to have a little one-on-one with you today, just talk about some stuff…"

He has me nervous.

"…and, Desiree, we work in a professional environment…"

Sure we do.

"…and your personal life is your business…"

Damn right it is. So, why the fuck are you talking about it?

"…but when it comes into the work place, I have to say something."

"I'm sorry," I said, shaking my head in confusion. "What, exactly, is coming into the workplace?"

He sighed and shifted in his seat, his voice dropping to a quiet tone that I really hated. "I was reviewing your call and I was able to see the inappropriate Instant Messenger exchange between yourself and Roland Dumas."

"Excuse me?" There was no way I had just heard that right.

"Look, Desiree, I'm on your side," Glen said. I barely resist screaming. "But, just try to keep conversations about your out-side activities a little more…private, in the future. Especially on company time and equipment…before this has to go to the next level."

Wow. Fucking wow.

He waited a minute before he gained the courage to speak. "Right now, this conversation is just between us, and I'd like to keep it that way," he told me, his voice dropping again. "I don't have to report it to HR unless this continues…" He paused. "This is a verbal coaching, and that's it. So just…make sure it stays that way." Glen offered me a smile as if that was supposed to make this okay. *Fat fucking chance.* "So," he said, blowing out a breath, leaning back in his chair. "Anything else you want to go over while you're here? How's the call volume been treating you?"

"Fine," I said quickly.

"No issues with burnout? Because there are always opportu-nities to move into other departments after six months to a year. Your calls are good and your stats are pretty solid—"

"I'm good, Glen. But thanks."

He nodded. "All right." He glanced at his clock. "Look, its five-fifteen now. Call volume is low, so why don't you go take an extra break on me, and we'll call the meeting over at five-thirty. Sound good?"

"Sure," I said, tapping my hands twice on the armrests before I rose and immediately turn to leave his office. I needed some damn air.

"Where you coming from? Seeing your boyfriend Roland?" Ahmad whispered.

"Ahmad. There's nothing going on between us," I said, waving my hand.

"That's what they all say," he mumbled, "including me. And if you like him, who gives a damn about in-office relationships?"

I rolled my eyes. "Lord Douchebag."

"Queen Bitchface. How are you, you okay?" Ahmad crossed his arms, as he sat in my desk chair.

"Fantastic. Now can you please get up?" Ahmad looked me in the eye as if he knew something was wrong, but didn't say anything. "Goddamn you, Ahmad!" I yelled. "What the hell was that?" He passed gas so loudly, it sounded like a ship's horn.

"Everything goin' all right over there?" a familiar voice asked.

"No, because Ahmad just," I paused, rolling my eyes in disgust. "Never mind, we're good, Kelly." I laughed.

"Sorry, it's the coffee I drank this morning," he mumbled. Then, I realized the rest of the team was staring at us, listening to our whole conversation, looking amused. Excluding Sheldon, who was on a call.

Over the next hour and a half or so, Ahmad, Lynette, and another coworker, Ron, spent their time talking about everything from retirement to favorite movies to dumb general political stuff. I sat in my seat in complete silence unless I was speaking with a customer. I was embarrassed that an incident such as this could happen—my manager seeing the explicit messages between Roland and me—I wanted to crawl under a rock.

"You okay?" Ahmad asked, as we both shut down our computers, logging off at the end of the day.

Chanel left two hours prior on personal time off, so I didn't mind speaking freely. "Not really, but we'll talk later.

"Something to do with your talk with Glen?"

"Yup." I stood, grabbed my keys, walked down the aisle before he could say anything else. I probably had my engine roaring out of the parking lot before Ahmad left his chair.

CHAPTER SEVEN

Roland

"Why do you always ask stupid questions?" Kelly was probing Ahmad with her eyes, taking note of every little detail of his facial expression. This shit is crazy. Kelly is being unprofessional, once again. She's on the production floor talking down to Ahmad in front of the other representatives. She did this exact same thing before, even after Ahmad threatened to contact Human Resources, but all Glen did was make her apologize. No repercussions. No warnings. Nothing.

Behind closed doors, Kelly and Michelle were always begging for help with questions because they didn't have a clue what was going on with everyday job functions of the representatives, but on the floor they exerted their power to intimidate, exclude, and belittle everyone.

From upper management down to lower management lacked communication. I didn't mind going over and beyond my job duties, but I despised laziness, and when I had to bust my ass to clean up other people's messes, and they act like they're entitled, that's where I had a problem. I worked hard every day. No raise. No promotion. No "Good job."

I respected Glen's hustle, but he really didn't care about much, as long as money was being made. My manager, Clarence, was very knowledgeable and knew his job, but he was a slob who was always late and left early. He never responded to emails, his favorite line was "You sent me something, when? I never received it," and getting him to sit down for a one-on-one meeting was impossible.

The majority of the management staff literally did minimal work. They stand in groups to talk and gossip while I, and a few other representatives on the escalation team, run around like chickens with our heads cut off, helping with questions, and taking escalated calls. Once the clock strikes five, and sometimes before that time, Kelly, Michelle, and Clarence would stop whatever they're doing, pack up all their belongings, and run out the door, even if the department was still a mess.

Kelly waited, as if expecting Ahmad to reply, but he said nothing. He turned and walked away, leaving her standing in the middle of the floor with a look of confusion. A few seconds later, my instant messenger flashed that a message was waiting.

5:15 PM Ahmad Mohammed: Can you come take this call? He's asking for a manager and there are no capable managers around.

5:16 PM Roland Dumas: Sure. On my way over there.

One of my job duties was to assist and provide training to the representatives. When I was not training, I worked the escalated calls queue, calls where the caller has requested to talk to someone higher up.

"What's going on?" I questioned Ahmad, as I walked up and began plugging into his phone line.

"To sum it up, his account is ninety days past due with no arrangements. He needs to use the card and I told him we need a payment and then he can use his card in about one to two days."

"What's his name?"

"*Getting on my nerves!*" Ahmad laughed. "No, it's Jason Wilson."

I get on the phone and give my normal speech. "Hi, Mr. Wilson, I understand that you have spoken to Ahmad and now you're requesting a manager. Is that correct?"

"Yes, that's correct." He sounded irritated. "I have explained my situation to the previous person and I need to know if you are the highest ranking person I can talk to because if not, put them on the phone because I'm not explaining it again." As Mr. Wilson continued to complain, I thought about what trouble I was going to get into when I got off work.

Ahmad was always being dramatic. As I talked to the customer on the phone, he walked over and grabbed a box from the supply area. Walking back to his desk, he began packing up all of his belongings.

As I tried to give the customer my full attention, I noticed Desiree had stopped what she was doing and began watching him.

"Ahmad," Desiree called out, as she picked up the papers Ahmad had dumped into the box. He ignored her, as he yanked open the cabinet drawer and began dumping items from the drawer into the box. "Now, Ahmad, this doesn't make any sense." Desiree said. "I didn't think you'd stoop this low and pack all your stuff." She shook her head and I shook mine, too.

"You don't understand." Ahmad laughed humorlessly "I'm sick and tired of these non-managing managers, talking mad shit all the time." Ahmad swallowed hard, as he grabbed a magazine from Desiree's desk, frowning as he flipped through the pages. "I'm about to be fired anyway. I have my sources so I know it's true." Ahmad turned to leave.

After I finished the call, I stood to walk away. "Where's Ahmad?" I asked curtly.

"In the break room," Desiree answered.

"What the hell is wrong with him?"I practically screamed. "He needs to stop acting off his emotions."

"He's had a bad day."

"Bad day, bad week, bad month …whatever. He needs to get over that,"

Desiree rolled her eyes and sighed.

Ahmad walked back to his desk and sat down.

"I already documented the account with the conversation I had with the customer. All you need to do is input your notes," I said to Ahmad.

He looked as if he had calmed himself down, probably after realizing he really needs this job.

"All right," he replied, and I began walking away.

"You good?" I overheard Desiree ask.

Ahmad cleared his throat. "Yeah, I just needed to get my thoughts together. But I need to take another break because I need a cigarette *bad*," I heard Ahmad say, as I listened from afar.

"So you're not quitting, right? Desiree inquired.

"Nope, not today, but don't be surprised if one day I don't show up."

I laughed and shook my head because Ahmad was hilarious with his daily dramatic antics.

After dealing with Ahmad's call, I went to the training room to finish up some paperwork. After two hours, I was the only one in the training room. It was getting late and I was about to head out when Tiara from my training class came strolling into the room around 7:25 p.m. Tiara and I were always flirting and secretly joking about what we'd do to each other if given the chance to be alone, but then again, she flirted with everyone in the class, so I didn't think too much about it.

"What are you doing here so late?" I inquired, startled by her sudden appearance.

"I think I left my wallet here, so I had to drive all the way back here from home." She winked while looking under papers at her station.

"How far do you live from here?" I said, trying to make small talk.

"About twenty minutes." She shook her head, smiling from ear to ear.

I was packing up my stuff. Once I had everything packed up, Tiara gave me that look. It was that *I want to fuck you* look.

"Find what you're looking for?" I asked in a flirtatious tone.

"Yup, right here." She turned down the lights, so only the faint lights in the room were on. Tiara closed and locked the door and wasted no time slipping out of her clothes.

I was completely aroused, as I watched her walk toward me in only her panty and bra. If caught, we both could be fired on the sport, but our desire had taken over and became our primary focus.

She knelt down and removed my shoes and socks before unzipping my pants, pulling them down along with my boxers. As they hit my ankles, she grabbed and lifted my dick and started sucking my balls. It felt amazing. She then took my dick inside her warm, wet mouth and slowly sucked my head, inching my dick deeper into her mouth until the tip of my dick touched her tonsil.

As she was sucking my dick, I removed my shirt and had her stand back up. I led her to the table in the middle of the room. I pulled off her panty and stuffed it in my pant pocket. I laid her down on the table. I could feel her heartbeat racing, and I was sure she could feel mine. As I entered her, she moaned softly, and wrapped her legs around my waist, and our fucking like rabbits ensued. I wanted a chance to fuck her and that chance came today. I wondered if everyone would smell our exploits tomorrow morning. Only time would tell.

I felt good, as my day ended on a high note. I walked out the building and as I approached my truck, I noticed someone standing up against it. My smile instantly turned into a frown. Trina's husband Dominic.

"Here we go again," I mumbled under my breath. "Is there a reason why you're standing by my truck?" I asked, as we stood in place, staring at each other for a few moments.

When he finally spoke, his voice was low and full of hurt. "Trina tried to hide her affair with you, said it was just text messages, nothing more." He paused. "She's been acting weird, discreet recently, coming home late or away on the weekend for some 'girl time'." He fidgeted with his cell phone, moving it from one hand to the other. "Claims she still loves me and that it was a mistake with you and she wants her family, but these text messages tell a different story."

This annoyed me for some reason. It wasn't helpful at all and completely obvious we weren't getting anything resolved. I looked at him, puzzled, as he continued to ramble on.

"I was able to get screenshots of text messages you two sent each other. It was so many, but I was able to capture one from March fifteenth at 2:04 p.m.

"You said, '*You look nice today. Thanks for sharing with me today.*'What she was sharing, I have no clue," Dominic exclaimed, shaking his head in disgust.

"Her response was, '*You're welcome, love. You need to know that I depend on you most amongst any man in my life. You listen to me and never judge me.*' Never judge, huh? I'm her husband, but she telling another man she depend on him, like I don't take care of my fucking household. Then there's a text from April third, starting at 10:57 p.m," he angrily blurted out

"You said, '*Your tongue game is real talented,*' and than *my* wife responded, '*I love you so much, I don't care who knows. I fall madly in love with you, more and more every day.*' I've had enough. I can't do this anymore." Dominic turned around, as if he was about to walk way, but turned back around. "The fucked up thing is," he said, his voice now tinged with intrigue, "that Trina is doing everything she can at home to try to make me believe she's so in love with me, but behind my back she's texting, saying how much she loves you. There were other text messages with her talking about how she had to move the baby seat to let the back seats down in *our* SUV, so that she could give you oral and have sex with you, in a vehicle I pay for." The more he spoke the angrier he became again.

I shook my head, but not in denial. I knew I deserved that tongue-lashing, but I didn't expect all of this drama. I guess neither Trina nor her husband knew that going through a person's stuff was one of the worst things a person could do in a relationship.

"We've been married for eight years and have four children."

My eyes widened, mouth hung open as I found myself at a loss for words. I looked at him as he talked about how hurt he was that his marriage was crumbling apart.

I looked around the parking lot to ensure no one was watching. "Bruh, listen to me for a minute. I have no intentions of being with Trina seriously, so you can have your marriage. No worries this way." If I told him what his wife and I did in the bedroom, his feelings would really be hurt. "Let me catch you up to speed. Your wife meant absolutely nothing to me."

Dominic's face turned bright red and his arms were shaking in fury, I thought he was just going to walk away but before I knew what was happening, he punched me right in my jaw with his fist. "You both will reap what you sow," he shouted while finally walking away. I stood there staring at him with a dumbfounded look on my face for probably a minute.

I waited until he got to his car. After he pulled off, I got into my truck and laughed for a few minutes. *This shit is getting out of hand*, I thought. I was fuming, but I kept a calm exterior because I knew my anger wasn't going to change things. I didn't think in a million years my situation with Trina would go this far.

Chapter Eight

Ja'Shay

I sucked in a deep breath, twiddled my fingers, and swallowed my courage, as Glen looked at me. It was now or never time on the honesty front, and I knew what I had to do.

"You're what?" Glen was puzzled.

"Pregnant. I'm pregnant, Glen. I…um… I wasn't on the pill," I admitted quickly.

"What?" he yelled, staring at me.

"I wasn't on the pill…"

Glen pushed back from his desk. "Are you fucking kidding me?"

Tears were building, but I willed them away, not wanting to break down in front of Glen. "I'm sorry," were the only words I could muster.

"How could you be so stupid?" he roared.

That did it. The dam broke, and tears flowed down my face. "I'm sorry. I'm sorry. I hadn't had sex for a long time, so I went off it, and I wasn't exactly expecting this to happen."

"This is fucking wonderful," Glen said, more to himself than to me. He stood from his chair and started pacing the floor of his office.

In response, my anger rose. "You should have used a fucking condom!" I would not allow him to place blame on me. It takes two to tango. "You didn't seem to mind at the time," I yelled. I came around to my senses. I did not make this child on my own! "So it was my fault neither of us used contraception?"

He stopped pacing. "Because I thought you were on the pill," he explained, using a slow, condescending voice. "I can't believe this." He began pacing again.

"You were there, too. It's not all my fault," I angrily spat.

Glen looked at me. "I can give you money to end it."

Appalled, shocked and downright angry, I snapped, "I won't kill *our* child, you selfish son of a bitch!"

Glen froze in place and stared at me. "You won't kill *your* child. I want nothing to do with this," he paused. "I am not about to marry you because you didn't use a contraceptive. And I'm not going to pay out my hard-earned money to care for a child that shouldn't be born. You keep this baby, Ja'Shay; you'll take care of it yourself."

And at that point, that was all my heart needed to hear before it started to crumble. "But, it's your child, too!"

"No. I was just a sperm donor. I don't want children, and will not allow you to force one on me. You were a one-night-stand. You were the forward one that night, so you should have at least had protection."

I cringed at the thought of my laying with him. "Why would I have protection when I had no idea I'd be having sex?"

When my period was late, I prayed it was because of stress. But it never came. I drove to Walgreen's and purchased several pregnancy tests. Every test came up positive. I didn't know what to do. Now I was three months pregnant and had decided to tell Glen he was about to be a father. I had hoped he would do the right thing and at least help take care of the child, but he was telling me *no*. He wasn't going to fulfill his responsibility. He wanted me to kill *our baby*. Well, I wouldn't do it.

"One minute my dick is in your mouth and the next you're riding me, and somehow in those few moments I was supposed to get my sex fogged brain to ask about protection. That's obviously a great way to get a guy to stick around." With every word he spoke, rage built within me. I wanted to scratch his eyes out, talking to me as if I were a twenty-dollar trick.

"I didn't expect to get pregnant, Glen!" I shouted, unaware that my anger was turning into rage. So as the heat in my body built and my heartbeat became louder in my ears, the rage continued to take over me, with clouded thoughts of a knife going through Glen's neck. Shaking my head, I dismissed those thoughts, grabbing my belly and silently praying to God that everything would work out in its own time. Motherhood called me and no matter what happened, Glen and I were forever connected by the life being created inside of me. *Our baby*.

Glen massaged the nape of his neck. "If you want this child, that's your choice. As I said, I want nothing to do with it...and if you try to force me, I will drag your name through the mud so deep it will leave a furrow that will encompass the entire building. No one will want to employ you when I'm done with you. So think hard about this, Shay," he said, scowling at me. "You can have children later when the father is ready."

I stood up. "Fine. I will raise this baby myself then. Why I thought you'd do the honorable thing is beyond me."

"It's beyond me, too. Now get out of my office. I don't want to hear another word about this child, *ever*."

"You fucking bastard!" I screamed, as I rose from my seat.

"You are exactly right. Good-bye, Miss Thompson," Glen said dismissively.

I stormed toward the door. "One day you're going to regret this," I mumbled. For a brief moment, as I grabbed the knob, I thought of how his words cut me, sliced through my soul, and made me feel as worthless as trash.

"I highly doubt that. Now get out of my sight. I am not above firing a pregnant woman," he said, staring at his computer.

As I caught the one single tear from escaping my eye, I mustered up some strength to respond. "Stupid bitch!" I cursed him and left his office. I took in a deep breath as the door slammed shut. *Selfish son of a bitch!*

I sat down in the break room and continued to think about Glen, the baby and myself. Since the day I found out I was pregnant, my stomach's inability to keep food down hadn't changed. I always thought morning sickness was delegated to mornings, but I was finding that most days, the vomiting could begin at any time, especially at night. Sleepless nights made me tired in the mornings. I typically felt better after throwing up, but it was the bouts of never-ending nausea that were getting to me. At my last doctor's appointment, I had actually lost weight, and though they said that was nothing to worry about in the short-term, I needed to work on keeping food down. I immediately attributed the weight loss to added stress.

No one at work had figured out I was expecting. I'd been staying low key, staying seated at my desk, only getting up for lunch, bathroom breaks, and mandatory meetings. I didn't want to stand out, announcing my pregnancy. Lately, I've been feeling like the walking dead and I knew I wasn't living up to my personal or professional standards.

Before I sat down to eat my lunch, I glanced around the break room and spotted Trina sitting with Veronica, my former best friend, and the two of them glanced over at me with concern. I sat down in an empty seat in the corner of the room and opened up a package of saltine crackers and a bottle of ginger ale. This had turned into my breakfast, lunch, and dinner. This baby wouldn't let me keep anything down but crackers and ginger ale. I smiled politely at a few coworkers at tables nearby, but pulled a book out of my bag in an attempt to avoid conversation. I could feel Trina's and Veronica's eyes on me again and I forced myself to focus on my lunch. I took a spoonful of yogurt and immediately regretted it. I spit it out into a napkin as unobtrusively as possible, and stuck with the crackers. Every now and then I'll try something different to see what my tummy would allow. This time was a fail.

Once upon a time, I would have joined Trina and Veronica and joked about the office gossip and may have even told them my big news. But I was afraid that once it was out, everyone's options of me would change. It was easier to avoid people than to face them. Lately, I'd been wondering why the opinions of others bothered me. I blamed the pregnancy and the range of emotions I went through daily. Of course, it had a lot to do with my previous spat with Glen as well.

My cell phone buzzed and I dug it out of my purse. Private number. I put the phone back inside my purse. I heard the scrape of a chair pulling up across from me. Clarence was sitting across the table, pulling out a chicken salad sandwich that smelled vile to my pregnant nose. I was about to excuse myself when he commented, "On a diet?" and pointed at my small meal. Once the words left his mouth, as if I had eyes in the back of my head, I felt Trina's and Veronica's eyes glaring at the back of my neck, like they couldn't wait for my answer.

"Yeah," I said curtly. It annoyed me that he would bring that up in front of everyone in the break room. I was fairly thin to begin with and I'd lost a few pounds recently due to the nausea. My weight was starting to move around a bit to accommodate the baby, but my shirts had just enough room in that I could still get them buttoned. I knew that it was only a matter of time before I'd be in the market for new clothes, but I wasn't there yet, and I couldn't believe he had that little tact to bring this up.

"My wife was on Weight Watchers," he said, his mouth full of sandwich. "She lost forty pounds. She's looking great. You should try that, much better than crackers."

My eyes welled with tears involuntarily. Even at my heaviest, which I hadn't seen since my college days when I'd drowned my sorrows in Ben and Jerry's on a few too many occasions, I had never had anywhere near forty pounds to lose.

Swallowing tears, I bitterly replied, "I'll try that." I gathered up my food as quickly as I could to get away from him and back to my desk before my eyes revealed my secret.

He seemed to get the tone of my comment and looked up apologetically. "Not that you need to lose…I mean…" His words trailed off as he lowered his head.

"I've got it…thanks," I muttered, pushing in my chair with a loud scrape and retreating toward my desk, feeling the stares of several coworkers on my back, including Trina and Veronica.

I found myself detouring to the bathroom for the third time that day, but fortunately, the crackers stayed down. My eyes weren't cooperating though and the tears began to roll down my cheeks. I knew it was insane, crying over the thoughtless comment of a coworker I didn't even like, let alone that he had no idea what was really going on. Hormones were raging and I couldn't get myself under control. I just kept thinking about what would happen when I did gain the weight, when the baby was noticeable, growing inside of me. Then the terrifying reality that I had no idea what I was doing. Right now, the baby was a distraction. In just a few months, it would be a reality that a person completely dependent upon me and I have no clue how to take care of a child. Nevertheless, even while life was growing inside me, I still considered myself a child when it came to the reality of life and living in it.

My cell phone buzzed again and I pulled it out of my purse, hoping it was an apology message from Glen, but it wasn't. Instead, it was a text message that read: Your Sprint bill is now past due, please contact Customer Service immediately by dialing #555 from your phone. I looked at my phone, and then threw it in my purse. "What else could go wrong?" I was so tired of allowing every single thing to get to me that I would normally brush off. It has to be the mood swings.

Now I am not a holy roller, by no means, but the only thing that was getting me through this was a lot of prayer and asking God to help me let it go. I'd always been a nervous, anxious person. I took deep breaths and realized that worrying would not fix anything, only make it worse. I tried to let go and trust God to make everything work out, and whatever happened, happened for a reason, but I kept thinking, *Why is he ignoring me? What's he thinking? Why isn't he talking to me? Why isn't he looking at me? Why isn't he calling me?*

Chapter Nine

Kelly

I plopped down at my desk while simultaneously shoving the last of a doughnut into my mouth. The calories didn't bother me since I had just spent the last forty-five minutes working out in the gym. I showered quickly and arrived at my desk just as the eight o'clock agents were walking in, a few early birds giving me polite "good morning" greetings as they passed on their way to their workstations. I nodded in return, as I opened my laptop and typed in my password to see if anything exciting happened overnight. If the sun didn't come up...blame Kelly. Everything that went wrong in this department always seemed to be my fault.

This was my daily routine and had been for the past few years. I always came in early, had a good work out, and caught up on emails while waiting for my team to come in to start the day. When the day was over, I was usually the first one out the door.

A few moments later, Chanel strolled in late and paused as if she were going to say something as she walked by my cubicle. I wasn't sure if she had noticed me or not...of course, she had, so I just watched her as I sipped coffee. She seemed lost in her thoughts and from the way she was chewing on her lower lip. I knew she was mad about something. She was always mad and complaining about something. Ahmad was saying something to make her to laugh.

"You know, watching someone the way you are could be construed as 'creepy'," Ahmad said, as he passed by my cubicle.

My left eyebrow arched, "Takes one to know one."

Ahmad grinned and shrugged. "Touché."

"Touché." I glanced up before I looked back down at my coffee cup.

"Hey, Shelly." Michelle smiled down at me. "You're not in a very good mood today, are you?" She stood outside my cubicle

"No, I'm not. My day is jam-packed and nothing is going my way."

"Talk about jam-packed, Glen sent me an email and wants me to create a team building exercise for the department. I don't have time for that." Michelle quietly giggled.

I was looking straight ahead, but I could see Michelle in my peripheral vision. "Have one of those overachieving agents on your team that will never be in management do it. Let them come up with some ideas and then you can present it to Glen."

"Good morning," said a voice outside my cubicle, making me jump.

"Good morning, Desi," Michelle and I said in unison.

I scanned the pool of mini cubicles in the middle of the production floor, looking for Ahmad. "Desiree, have you seen Ahmad?" I asked on my way out of the cubicle.

"He's in Glen's office."

I closed my eyes and took a deep breath. Was the universe out to make my life one big struggle today? I collected myself before walking over to Glen's office. I knocked firmly on the door and entered, not waiting for an answer.

Glen's eyes darted to me, startled. "Oh, I'm sorry. I must not have heard myself call you in," Glen said seriously, although his eyes revealed a teasing glint. I was not amused. I looked at Ahmad, who sat in front of Glen's desk.

Deliberately not giving Glen the satisfaction of acknowledging his obnoxious comment, I turned to Ahmad. "Sorry for interrupting, are you okay, Ahmad? I actually came in here because I need you back on the phones. We have a lot of calls holding." I wanted to slap that condescending little smirk right off Ahmad's face.

"Yes, everything is okay. I just wanted to speak with Glen about a few things. I guess that's now all right with you, since you came looking for me." Ahmad looked up at me. "That reminds me, could you please refrain from telling everyone in the office that you hate me?"

"I've never told anyone that I hate you," I said, my face the picture of innocence.

Ahmad raised his eyebrows at me. "It was brought to my attention that you said you hoped that I made a mistake on my calls so you could walk me out the door."

I bite back laughter.. "I never said that." I lied "But that doesn't necessarily mean I hate you. People around here are always jumping to conclusions." A knock on the door prevented Ahmad from responding.

"Come in!" Glen called, breaking the tension that was growing in the office. Ja'Shay walked into the office. Glen looked up at her. "What can I do for you?" he sternly asked.

"I'll come back. I just wanted to speak with you for a moment."

I tapped Ahmad on the shoulder, we slipped out of Glen's office, and I headed straight for the cafeteria.

"You don't think the rumors about Ja'Shay and Glen are true?" I leaned into the table and whispered.

"No," Michelle replied quickly. "Ja'Shay and Glen can't be dating. Ja'Shay isn't Glen's type, is she? There's no way that's possible."

"Right," I said. "Glen likes girls who are slender and athletic, and Ja'Shay is too… curvy for that. Plus, I didn't know Glen dated Black girls."

Michelle crossed her legs and ate a piece of bacon before leaning forward. "I mean, she may have a flat stomach as I do, but her hips are too wide and her thighs are too large. Plus, she's way too top heavy and Glen told me that he prefers a more manageable size on women." Michelle looked around slyly. Confident that no one was eavesdropping, she continued. "You know, she's rather large in her butt area for someone so skinny in others."

I nodded in agreement. "Something's going on. I saw the two of them exchanging not so pleasant words in the parking lot two days ago."

Michelle knew all about work relationships that go wrong. She had a semi-serious relationship a few years ago with a previous coworker, Ron. She even considered marrying Ron, even though he was verbally and physically abusive to her. I mean, that's true love right there, I guess. But then Ron was fired and Michelle began to feel suffocated by Ron's affection. He was always finding a way to show up here at work. On several occasions, the police were called because he showed up here at the job drunk, cursing and threatening Michelle in front of anyone that was in ear distance. Michelle decided to end their relationship.

Apparently, Ron wasn't taking *no* for an answer. He began inventing insane stories to try to see Michelle, including claiming his mother was dying and him seriously injured in a car accident. He even tried to break into her home while she was asleep. In other words, he went more than a little insane. At one point, she had to live with me and my family for two weeks until Ron was finally arrested.

"Ladies!"

I spun around to find Clarence standing behind our table. My eyes narrowed slightly. How did I miss him when I was looking around? "Good morning Clarence, how are you?"

"Good morning, troublemakers." Clarence slightly chuckled.

"We weren't 'bad-mouthing' anybody," I said. "How do you know what we were talking about anyway?" I laughed, trying to cover up my embarrassment.

"I actually didn't hear the conversation. You both just look guilty. Whatever it is, it's their business and not the business of two managers, who, by the grace of God, just got out of another situation that included gossip." Clarence away from our table.

"What are you talking about?" I snapped, noticing a few faces turn with curiosity. I took a few breaths to calm myself as I spot Ahmad and Chanel, both on an unauthorized break, walk out of the cafeteria with takeout containers in hand. "I can't wait to get rid of both of them," I blurted, as Michelle and I finished our breakfast.

I walked back to my desk and motioned for Desiree to gather everyone for our meeting. Everyone gathered around my desk as I pulled out my 'to do' list that I jotted down on a yellow sticky note.

"Good morning. We only have a few minutes, so I will make this quick. I have certain expectations I expect you all to follow. I'm going to keep this as simple as possible. If anyone has additional questions, you can speak with me one-on-one.

"First, you all must retain control of your tone during conversation you are having with customers. Next, proper hygiene and the dress code are not suggestions. Follow them. Unauthorized breaks will not be tolerated. Adhere to your assigned break schedules. Unlimited overtime is being offered until further notice and, lastly, some of you may have noticed, but due to unfortunate circumstances, Tsuki was let go yesterday." There were a few gasps and groans.

"Oh, Lord, if they can get rid of the mute one, I don't stand a chance," Ahmad joked.

After the meeting I walked over to Glen's office and saw Clarence leaving, so I knew he was alone. Glen's office door was open and he was sitting at his desk, looking through some reports.

"Hey, you." Glen looked up and smiled. "Is there something going on between you and Ja'Shay you're not telling me?" I joked, being nosey.

"There is nothing going on, we're just dealing with this little situation." Glen shook his head.

"What do you mean?" I was becoming more intrigued by the second. He looked up at me and then stared past me. "Are you okay? You totally zoned out on me for a second," I asked with concern

Glen laughed. "I'm okay, just a lot on my mind."

The conversation remained scarce. I wondered how I could get Glen to open up, without being obvious. This was harder than I first anticipated. He decided to break the ice. I guess he couldn't take this awkwardness anymore.

"Kelly, did you come here for a reason?" he asked, trying to sound nonchalant.

I was startled by the question; I didn't expect him to be so direct.

"Yes, I did," I admitted looking at him

"Well?" he asked impatiently.

"I told my team about Tsuki being let go. There were mixed reactions. We discussed call abandonment and the no tolerance policy for initially hanging up on customers."

"Seventy-five calls in one month, that's ridiculous. We hired her to collect not hang up on people."

"Guess no one believes that reports do exist."

"Or they just don't care."

"Also, is there anything I need to address with Ahmad after you two met this morning?" I asked, as I stood to leave.

"Nope, he's just going to be one of those individuals who always complain and always have something to say."

After I left Glen's office, I remembered I needed to speak with Chanel once regarding a complaint made against her from a customer. I tapped Chanel on the shoulder, letting her know I wanted to speak with her.

"Now what?" She huffed and puffed, as she slammed down her headset.

We both walked into the small conference room. I wasn't shocked by the attitude. I've known Chanel over four years.

Chanel and I sat facing each other, in awkward silence; neither knew what to say to the other.

"What happened between you and that customer yesterday?" I asked.

"Nothing, why?" Chanel looked up at me.

"You were very disrespectful." I tried to keep it professional, but Chanel had a way of bring the worst out of me. "I pulled the call and listened."

"Okay, so you know what happened."

I was done with playing nice. "Chanel, I'm going to put it on the table, and I think your attitude is setting you up to be fired." I was getting annoyed. Instead of this being a one-on-one conversation, it was turning into a shouting match. "Do you realize how rude you were?"

"No I wasn't; they called to make a payment. He was calling me out of my name throughout the entire conversation. I told him on several occasions not to talk to me like that and he continued and I disconnected the call." Chanel's mouth dropped opened and her eyes were starting to water. Of all the arrogant, presumptuous, and foul things she has said to everyone, the mentioning of her possibly being fired and now she wanted to cry. Chanel screwed up her face in disgust. "You make it sound like you already have something planned to get rid of me."

"No, I don't have anything planned."

"You play favoritism anyway, but it's not my place to convince you otherwise. I can only give you my opinion, and it's that. Rumor around the floor is that you and Glen are looking to get rid of people for any and everything."

"Rumors are just that, rumors. Don't believe everything you hear; always check the source."

"You're clearly delusional." Chanel said. "No one likes you, Kelly. You're hard to work with. Take a look around, about ten people left the team and department over the course of three years due to bad treatment from you." There were a few moments of silence. Chanel gave me a smirk before she stood up and walked out the conference room.

I walked slowly out of the conference room and was ready to end my day. As I walked by, I overheard a conversation a few of my representatives were having. At first, I was going to ignore them, but I heard my name and my curiosity got the best of me, so I hid behind a pillar, and I listened.

"Kelly is never around for us anymore," Ahmad said.

"When was the last time she gave us positive feedback? It's always about something we're doing wrong," Desiree chimed in.

"One would expect she would at least try to learn her job. It's like she doesn't care for us," Shelton added

I stood there frozen, filling up with anger. I knew not everyone would like me as a manager, but overhearing a conversation in which my own representatives insulted me struck me hard. If my staff had a problem with me, they could tell me. I could accept criticism and act reasonably fair to people who came with legit issues. But being insulted and gossiped about behind my back felt treacherous and lame.

At first I wanted to stormed over and interrupt their conversation, explain to them how hard I worked to keep Glen off their backs and helped secure their jobs. I had actually created a whole speech in my head, but I didn't have to explain myself to them. I walked around the corner and stood outside of my cubicle.

"Everything's okay?" I forced a smile, as tears welled in my eyes.

CHAPTER TEN

Chanel

I don't know how much more I can take. I was stressed, tired, and overwhelmed dealing with problems at home with my kids. I've been at work a little over an hour and everyone was getting on my damn nerves. When I logged into my work email, I had a few unanswered messages, including an email from Kelly.

Chanel,

It's been brought to my attention that there have been issues with you and several other representatives in the department, and also when transferring calls to other departments. We've discussed this before, and you seem to struggle with accepting feedback. Chanel, you're not being a team player and your peers could view this as a threat. I would like to meet with you later today to discuss this in more depth.

Thank you,

Kelly

Kelly was good for bringing up old stuff. That incident with my not accepting feedback happened months ago.

"Chanel?"

Of course I heard Kelly calling my name but I didn't care, I was livid with her. How dare she speak to me as if I'm a little kid during our weekly team meeting about how I'm not performing to my fullest potential? I felt like this was something she should have discussed with me in private, so I snapped on her and then stormed out the room.

"Chanel!" Kelly shouted for the millionth time, as she rushed behind me.

I was furious. Never in my life have I met such a bitch, a name I was two seconds from calling her.

"Kelly, I think it is best you leave me alone right now," I yelled.

"Chanel, stop!"

I ignored her and kept walking.

"That bitch truly wrecks my last fuckin'—" I stopped speaking and took a couple of deep breaths to ease my nerves, and mentally gave myself a pep talk. *You'll be fine. Just be cool, be polite, and don't say anything too out the box.*

"Who? What happened?" Desiree inquired.

Ahmad and Desiree looked at one another nervously. My eyes went from Shelton to Desiree and back to Shelton. "Dumb bitch," I said angrily. "The only thing she is good at is saying: *I'll research that for you, give me a moment.* Bitch I don't have a moment I have the customer on the phone now."

Ahmad shushed her. "Girl, you might want to watch what you say. Word is you're on your way out…"

I read out loud the email that Cruella De Ville, aka Kelly, sent.

Sheldon looked stunned, but remained silent while Ahmad tried to calm me down.

"See, this is the exact reason why I've been trying to keep you calm and stay focused to avoid things like this," Ahmad explained

I struggled against my emotions for a moment as I thought it over. "I'm willing to keep my mouth shut because of you, but she is always nitpicking about something," I said, looking over at Ahmad. I could see how much he really cared just by his eyes.

"You better lower your voice. You know she can hear everything," Ms. Goody Two-Shoes Desiree added.

"You're keeping your mouth shut because you need your J-O-B and the coins it provides every two weeks," Ahmad said sarcastically.

I shifted my gaze away for a moment and then quietly said, "Fuck you."

Ahmad rolled his eyes upward. "Do you?"

I nodded. "Yes." We both laughed. That brief laughter we shared reaffirmed that I had people in my life that cared and wanted to see me do well.

"Why don't you try talking to Glen about her attitude?" Desiree offered.

Glen is the department manager, a demanding and rude asshole, and I've worked for him for a little over four years now. He's the most irritating and arrogant man I had ever met. He's pompous, self-righteous, and bossy. Half the time I have trouble refraining from slapping him across the face, so I avoid any contact with him at all cost. All the other women in the office didn't seem to despise him as much as I did. They would boast about how good-looking he was for a white man, how so accomplished he was for his age. Tall, seemingly self-confident, always dressed in what appears to be designer suits, with his usual over-the-top colored ties. His hair, dark with a copper tinge, was always sleek and combed back behind his ears, and his bright grey eyes were always looking down on you constantly, like you were little more than something unpleasant stuck on his polished leather shoes.

"Last time I spoke with Glen I felt like I was talking to a brick wall. His none personality having ass don't really give a fuck about what goes on around here except numbers. As long as the department numbers look good at the end of each month he's all good," I replied, as my breath grew louder and I grew angrier. I wasn't going to let this pass.

Kelly's and my work relationship started out well, but it didn't last long. We've worked together for the last four years. She used to come to work, speak, say "Hi," shoot the breeze, and talk about her family and kids. She was a very friendly person.

Now she was extremely unprofessional. She talked and gossiped all day. Whenever I tried to ask her for help, she didn't budge to assist. Now all she cared about was herself. If she wasn't such a bitch and was a little more humble, we could probably get along better. She was always angry and, in her delusional mind, she was always right. I refused to give her any respect because she didn't give me any.

I wondered when karma was going to kick Kelly in the ass. I was very overwhelmed and on edge at all times. She disciplined me for things she didn't discipline anyone else for, but because it's *me* she thought she could do it. It's crazy. I even wondered if there was a vendetta against me.

Yesterday afternoon she sent me an email asking me what time I punched out at the end of my shift on Sunday because Michelle said she saw me off the phone and saying 'goodbye' two minutes before my shift ended. Mind you, I was certainly not the only person who was off the phone early. But maybe that was my issue, keeping the focus on me. I replied to her email, stating that I didn't remember; it was three days ago. So now she was going to pull my log-in/log-out report and if there were multiple instances of my logging off early, I could be written up or, depending on the severity, terminated.

It truly was a hostile work environment. I felt sick to my stomach. Having the log-in/log-out report and this email about my not being a team player over my head, I dreaded going into the office again and facing that bastard, Glen. I'd had enough right now. I was calling in sick tomorrow. Kathy, a representative on our team, had been out of work for almost two months due to stress and anxiety, thanks to Kelly. She was trying to get disability, good for her. I might have to look into that for myself.

Chapter Eleven

Glen

I t had been a shitty day…a long, shitty day. I'd never been more grateful to be off work. Normally, I enjoyed coming to work, but lately work had become the equivalency of hell! Every day there was an incident: sexual harassment, worker incompetence, bitching and complaining from the representatives, meetings that lasted longer than required, Human Resources up my ass about yearly performance appraisals being late, and the list goes on.

For the first time in my career, I wondered if this was the right job for me. I rubbed my eyes as prepared to leave the office. After shutting down my computer, I grabbed my jacket and messenger bag, making sure I had everything I needed: iPhone, laptop, keys, wallet…yep, got everything! Heading out of my office, I shuffled my feet across the horrendous carpet of the hallway that led to the elevators. I jabbed my finger against the call button a million times, wishing for the elevator to come up quicker so I could go home.

Finally! No one gets on the elevator, but me and I'm glad I didn't have to socialize with anyone. Some people could be so talkative and I was not in the mood to deal with people at this moment. I exited the building and made my way through the parking lot to my car. I inhale deeply. Despite being the winter season, the air was warm and fresh smelling. It had snowed earlier, but the sky had cleared and there was a spectacular sunset. Rolling my shoulders to release the tension I'd been holding, I used the key remote to unlock the door and got in.

I was looking forward to getting home and unwinding. I was hoping for this day to end well with no traffic, but my wish did not come true. On the busy intersection, as I pulled out of the parking lot, there was an accident that wasn't even so bad, but that didn't stop the Lookie-loos, slowing their asses and everyone else's down. It took over twenty minutes for me to go one mile in the six o'clock traffic jam.

When I made it past the accident, traffic picked up. I pulled into the hole in the wall bar with the shitty jukebox and scuffed table located a few blocks from the job. It wasn't an upscale bar, so despite my tailored suit and designer shoes, I fell right into place. I would have been happier in jeans and a sweatshirt, but dressing appropriately was a necessary part of my job.

I found an empty spot near one end of the bar and took a seat. I had hardly even taken my seat before the bartender was asking for my drink order.

"Whiskey straight up, please."

"Of course," he replied with a wink.

I rolled my eyes when he turned away.

I was halfway through my drink when I saw her. I caught a glimpse of her in the mirror behind the bar and I nearly knocked my glass over in shock. Marilyn Sullivan.

Annoyed, I tossed back the rest of my drink and reached for my check to pay for it. I wanted to get out of there and head home. I signaled for the waiter and rummaged through my wallet for some cash. When I looked up, he had placed another whiskey in front of me.

"I didn't order that. I actually wanted my bill."

"No charge. It's from the female at the end of the bar." My head snapped up and my eyes met the female that was staring at me through the mirror. She lifted her drink and winked. I nodded to her as I picked up the drink. I paid for my first drink. When I turned around to leave, Marilyn, the managing Director of Human Resources from work, was invading my personal space.

Startled, I wobbled a little on my feet. With a slow smirk, she grabbed my upper arm to steady me. "Careful, handsome."

"Thanks." I smiled as her hand slowly moved from my shoulder to my arm.

"You aren't leaving, are you?" Marilyn asked not even trying to hide her teasing smile.

"I am." I stood to leave. I stared in her face. She looked unchanged. I became engaged in my thoughts. I missed her heavy perfume, even though I hated the smell because it made me sneeze. I missed her glaring and her exasperated sighs. I missed the high energy she brought everywhere she went and I missed when I was too drunk to do much but let her help me into bed.

Once we were official, our relationship moved rather quickly, and it was a matter of a month or two before I was practically living with Marilyn, caught up in new love. Actually, I became complacent in our relationship and living arrangements that I accepted her habits and quirks as part of her personality and ignored what was really happening.

My life became controlled in almost every way. Marilyn was constantly at my side, always in my office at work and wanted to be involved in every detail of my life outside of our home and work. She checked calls and messages on my phone and when I made or received calls, she was somewhere listening and asking questions. I nearly gave up talking to anyone other than when I was at work and she wasn't around. I barely went out anymore and my friends and I began drifting apart.

I didn't understand how things between us went downhill so quickly. One day we were happy, heading down the path of love and the next minute we were having huge arguments that led to the demise of our yearlong relationship. Marilyn didn't accept the break up without a lot of yelling, name-calling, crying, begging, threats, and middle-of-the-night phone calls and surprise visits to my office. I found it hard to refrain from making snarky comments about her because she was bringing chaos into the workplace.

"Are you sure I can't convince you to stay and have another drink?" She pouted, and it was adorable. I wanted to take her lower lip between my teeth.

I took a swallow of my whiskey. I was fairly certain if given the chance she could convince me to do just about anything. "No, it's been a long day. I just want to get home."

She stepped closer to me and leaned in to speak quietly in my ear. "I can think of a great way to help you unwind."

I turned my head slightly until our mouths were just inches apart. "Oh yeah?"

"Yeah. Maybe start with another drink…"

I shrugged, acting completely indifferent. "All right, a drink. But I promise nothing beyond that."

She smirked at me again. "Trust me, you'll be feeling much better by the time we're done with drinks."

She leaned in to order another round from the bartender and I took a moment to examine her. She was still absolutely lethal. I'd never seen anyone else like her walk through that building in the ten years it had been since we started working together. Suddenly, I wanted to take advantage of the situation we were in—tease her, seduce her, and then leave her wanting more. Delicious revenge after all the years I'd spent panting after her sexy, chocolate body.

I took her arm after she'd acquired our drinks and I led us to a secluded table in the corner. I reveled in knowing her eyes followed every little movement I made. Hearing a familiar, cloying laugh, I glanced around the room and spotted Veronica, Roland, Ahmad, Desiree, Shelton, and Clarence sitting at a table in the back of the room. The table was a mess: napkins, beer bottles, and plates were everywhere, and whatever Ahmad was talking about caused everyone to laugh. I excused myself and walked over to speak.

"*Hey*, what's up, guys?" I greeted, as I approached the table.

"Hey, Glen, glad you could join us," Sheldon said. "Have a seat, stay a while."

"Hey, Glen," everyone at the table screamed out with laughter.

I declined the offer. "Enjoy yourselves, and don't get too drunk. I need you all at work tomorrow." I turned toward my table.

Walking back to where Marilyn was patiently waiting was when thoughts of our last group outing: my being drunk and creating a child I had absolutely no interest in—emotionally or financially.

Chapter Twelve

Desiree

I sat in the parking lot, staring at Roland's Hummer parked a few spots down. I watched him closely, never taking my eyes off him, not even chancing a blink. If I did, even for one split second, I felt like I'd miss something about him; any sort of subtle change. By now, I knew his every movement—the shaking of his head as he spoke to someone, the way his broad shoulders shook up and down from his melodious laugh, the subtle wrinkles at the corner of his eyes when he was deep in thought. I knew it all. I'd memorized him intently, analyzed him for far too long. His bright smile, his warm eyes, his overall likeable personality took him to another level. He had a way of engaging everyone around him, and I was no different from anyone else. I was captivated by his mere presence, even now, as I watched him step out of his truck and walk toward the building.

To say I was obsessed with him was way off base and, quite frankly, an insult to me. I didn't have some sort of silly high school crush on him where I watched him from afar, hoping he'd make the first move. No, this was different. First off, I was an adult and quite capable of expressing my feelings in a mature and respectable manner. Second of all, I loved the way he made my body feel.

I shook my head at myself and pulled my keys out of the ignition, putting them in my pocket before I forced myself out of my car. I swipe my badge and walk inside, strolling in at a comfortable 9:53 a.m. I'm a little grouchy, probably because I'm hung over after drinking away my weekend with Ahmad. He was happy to participate in my drinking binge because I was spilling my whiny little guts to him about Roland and me having sex the previous Thursday in the locker room shower at work.

Roland dared me to try something different sexually and I'm never one to turn down an opportunity to try something new. Shit went down fast, the location Roland chose was the most uncomfortable five minutes I've ever experienced, the space was built for only one person but I can't complain because overall it was a great experience. Ahmad listened as I cried about how stupid I felt about the whole thing, and instead of giving me crap about it and calling me the hoe that I felt like, he told me that if it had been him, he'd have done everything the same.

Since I woke up this morning, everything seemed a little off; I'm not sure what it is yet just different. My heartbeat accelerated exponentially. Roland was looking at me as we both stood waiting for the elevator inside the building. One corner of his mouth began to turn up into a playful smile, causing the air inside me to whoosh out in a longing sigh. Before I knew what was happening, he was walking over to me, one shiny black shoe in front of the other. I began to inwardly panic. What do I do? What do I say? What does he want? Do I look all right?

"Hi," Roland greeted, his playful smirk always making me forget how to breathe.

"Hi, I replied. I was amazed that I could even talk to him. Sometimes I'd even forget my name around this man.

His eyes dropped down, and I frowned at the loss of connection. "Since when did you start drinking coffee?" he asked, chuckling.

"You're late, I drink coffee every morning." His eyes swiftly roamed down my figure before landing on my face again. My entire body shivered in delight.

"You look nice today," he remarked, leaning against the elevator. I'd decided today to wear a deep pink cardigan and a form fitting gray pencil skirt, my hair pinned up in a bun. I'd taken extra care to appear more done up than usual in hopes that he would say something like that. Mission accomplished.

"Thank you," I replied timidly. "You do, too." He always looked amazing. He was wearing a black polo sweater with a white shirt and multi-color tie beneath. He was like something out of a GQ magazine. He had swag for days.

He flashed his perfect teeth at me, "I'll message you," he said, and winked at me before we both walked off the elevator headed in two separate directions. When I walked on the production floor, the chatter was more intense, voices rattling off account numbers faster than normal and when I check, the monitors are blaring red with an obscene amount of calls holding.

"Good morning, Ahmad," I say strolling to my desk five minutes before ten, falling casually into my seat I log into my phone before I swivel my chair, facing him. I am not going to look at her. Nope. Not gonna. I take a bite of my bacon, egg, and cheese biscuit from Hardee's, and my eyes dart to the right and then back forward.

"Good morning, Chanel," I say quietly, it takes her a second after I speak before her red heels slowly make their way in my direction. I see from my peripheral vision as she shrugs out of her coat and hangs it on the back of her chair, but then she changes her mind and folds it up, placing it in her bottom drawer.

"Hi Desiree," she says, trying to sound cheerful, but it's too forced and it doesn't fool me. "Good morning, Ahmad," I overhear Chanel say while I fire up my computer. "How was your weekend?" she adds as I take a sip of my coffee and try not to listen, scanning my emails and praying there's one from Kelly that says I passed my quality for the month.

"Nothing too wild. How was yours?" Ahmad replies. I couldn't hear Chanel's response because she was facing the inside of her cubicle talking to Ahmad. "Turnt," Ahmad said, with a chuckle and I peeked over my shoulder at him, but my sight snagged on Chanel smiling at him.

I cleared my throat. "Since neither of you have noticed," I snapped and pointed to the monitors that were lit up with calls holding, "we're too busy for swapping campfire tales right now." I jerked on my headset and hit my Auto In button, praying we continued to be over flooded with calls for the rest of forever because I had no desire to listen to Chanel's old ass talking about turning up anymore.

"Ol' nasty bitch," Ahmad mouthed at me with laughter

"Miss me," I taunt muting my phone as I pucker a kiss at him, "Good morning, this is Desiree..." My eyes dart toward the monitors, and my stomach drops as the numbers continue to climb.

At almost forty years old, Chanel is always talking nonsense about certain people at work and on Facebook, but claims to be a God-fearing woman. She would cause drama on herself because nobody at work, not even the supervisor, was being nasty to her. I wish she would just quit.

Like when she was talking to Ahmad about a weekend she needed off that was denied by Kelly, complaining about how it wasn't right.

"Why were you denied?" Ahmad asked her.

"Kelly claims there is no coverage, but when I checked it was hours in the system."

Chanel felt like there was a huge conspiracy going on at work that only affected her. She rambled on about how mad she was and that she didn't get the weekend off because of some personal hatred Kelly has for her.

"Chanel, I don't think that it's that at all. We are short staffed on weekends. We all know if you put a weekend request in less than two weeks in advance it can be denied based on the amount of people who work," I added.

Chanel rolled her eyes at me like she often rolled her eyes and spoke to me like I was a complete idiot. Sometimes, she wouldn't speak to me all day and pretended I didn't exist. We were in a phone queue and it seemed like I took all the calls that she wouldn't take because she was always off the phone complain about something. Yet, she claimed she was overwhelmed. I wanted to hurt my manager for sitting me next to her.

"I didn't ask for your input," Chanel snapped at me, "I was talking to Ahmad."

"Calm down, boos," Ahmad, the workplace mediator, said.

This was already a high stress, fast-paced job, so I didn't need the additional ignorance and arrogance from Chanel when I got up every goddamn morning to make a dime. She was so dead set on thinking people were picking on her, she just wouldn't see anything in a rational light. I truly believed she just wasn't happy unless she designed some form of drama. I really wished she would leave, but I knew that wouldn't happen any time soon.

The rest of the day was a blur. Call after call after call, and I don't remember a single detail of any of the trillion calls I took. Talking to Roland via instant messenger was the highlight of my day.

Chapter Thirteen

Glen

I took a minute to stare at the concrete structure before me. It was depressingly mundane, a cement walkway leading up to glass-encased double doors. Tall enough to encompass three floors, three stairwells, and one elevator shaft, the front of the building was a grid of concrete, filled in with glass panels that reflected the surrounding office building. Prominently displayed on the side of the building was the company's name in Optima typeface.

I blinked before opening the door and starting another day at the office. The walk to my office always instilled dread. I never knew why, it was just one of those things that deserved to be dreaded. Maybe I feared getting pulled over and talked to by a representative about something I wasn't interested in, or maybe I just dreaded coming to work.

In the swift four minutes it took to get to my office, nothing extraordinary happened. I wasn't pulled aside by a representative or manager. Setting my briefcase underneath the desk, I reluctantly pulled several papers out of it before booting up my computer. I tiredly laid the papers on my desk, staring at them for several minutes before turning to my computer.

ERROR IN BOOT PROCESS. INSERT BOOT DISK AND RESTART.

"What the hell?" My eyes narrowed. My fingers hit the classic CTRL-ALT-DEL keys in an attempt to fix it. I knew it wouldn't, but there was no harm in hoping.

ERROR IN BOOT PROCESS. INSERT BOOT DISK AND RESTART.

The message glared at me from the other side of the black screen. Shaking my head, I reached down under the desk to hit the power button to restart the machine.

"Piece of—"

ERROR IN BOOT PROCESS. INSERT BOOT DISK AND RESTART.

"—shit." I took a deep breath, trying to end the anger that was starting to rise up in my throat.

"Good morning, boss man. What's goin' on?"

I greeted Kelly with a head nod.

I frowned. "My computer's acting flaky."

"What's it doing?" Kelly walked around my desk.

"It says I need to insert a boot disk to continue booting. But I don't have a boot disk."

Kelly frowned. "Call tech support." She shrugged "I hate messing with these machines. They might get you a new one."

I nodded. "All right"

Kelly walked off, but turned around. "I will have my reports to you in about twenty minutes. You should probably go to the tech manager for that booting issue, it will be quicker."

I sighed as she stepped out of my office.

I sat at my desk lost in thought, with a cup in my hand, my fingers twitching nervously as a look of agony masked my face. I was pale, paler than usual; my eyes looked weary and black bags were developing underneath my eyes.

I brought the cup to my lips and slowly drank the liquid content. When I drank the contents, I tasted a strange flavor. It was cold, yet sweet and light....White Chocolate Mocha from Starbucks, my favorite. I sat the cup down on the desk and stared at the two empty chairs in front of me. The feeling of hollowness filled me to the brim.

A huge smile crossed my face when a text message from Marilyn popped up. Our night together a few weeks ago was full of laughter, reminiscing, and lots of sex. By the time I got home, it was nearly five in the morning. I was physically and emotionally exhausted, and burning with shame at how far I had gone beyond what I had planned to be my limits. I left her house with a hangover that I couldn't begin to describe; I thought I was dying. I felt so bad, my teeth even hurt.

I closed my eyes for a few moments. I took a few deep breaths and tried to relax until my cell phone began making that weird buzzing sound again, alerting me I had a text message. It was Ja'Shay letting me know she was back from her doctor's appointment and if I was interested in knowing what they said she would update me.

Barely a month had passed since Ja'Shay told me she was pregnant, but it felt like mere days.

"Pregnant! How could I be that fucking careless?" I muttered, as I brought my hand up to my face, wiping the liquid that threatened to form tears. *Your life is over,* a voice echoed in my head. *Why didn't you wear a condom?* I plugged my ears and pressed my face against the cherry wood desk.

"Fuck!" I screamed. I kicked the chair in front of me and pounded my fist onto the desk. The cup on my desk bounced from the powerful pound and spilled all over the desk. I stood up, rubbing the back of my neck. I needed to release my emotions. The anger that suddenly filled me, the sadness I felt, was tearing my heart apart. I pounded on my desk once again, harder than before. I continued to punch the desk, brushing aside the pain it caused. At this point, I didn't care who heard all the commotion. With more power I tightened my left fist and swung my arm down on the desk with more force.

"Bitch!" I stood and now began punching the wall, instantly knocking off the pictures that hung the wall.

Kelly knocked a picture off the wall as she rushed through the door. "You okay?" she shockingly asked, while scanning the office, looking at sharp, shattered glass all over the floor.

"Ugh!" I screamed, as I stumbled back and clasped my left arm across my chest. I looked down at my hand and glared at the flow of blood coming from my knuckles. I tried to move my wrist, but a stinging pain stopped me from moving it any further. I slumped down to the floor, gasping for air as Kelly picked up the phone and dialed 911.

"Calm down, it's going to be okay. I called security and 911," Kelly spoke through my heavy breathing.

I closed my eyes as if I were fading away. I could feel my arm numbing. I allowed my injured arm to drop down to my side as the memory of that drunken night with Ja'Shay bolted my memory like lightning.

"I fucked up," I mumbled, as I leaned back onto Kelly who was now sitting beside me on the floor. I felt my eyes water once more, but I made no attempt to stop the tears from flowing down my cheeks.

"Kel." I felt her head lean against my shoulder.

"It's going to be okay," Kelly whispered and gently kissed my head. She slowly pushed me back against the wall as my eyes met her. "What did you do?" was the last thing I heard before I saw complete darkness.

"Glen! Glen!" There was a male voice I didn't recognize right away, and then a female voice that sounded familiar. "*Glen?*"

Then there were hands – tapping my face, firmly but gently, then the throbbing started, and I briefly wondered if I would die. Unfortunately, another, more demanding voice chose that moment to break through the fog.

"Glen! Open your eyes!" That was a voice I definitely recognized, one that refused to be ignored. Knowing I couldn't disobey an order from Marilyn, my eyes slowly fluttered open. There were three faces staring down at me: Kelly, Clarence, and Marilyn.

Where am I? Why is there a freight train tearing through the back of my head? I thought as the presence of Kelly and Clarence reminded me I was at work and not at home. "Kelly?" I mumbled, hardly recognizing my own voice. "Kelly?" Now I was starting to panic. But when I tried to sit up, three sets of hands stopped him.

"Whoa, Glen," Clarence said. "Where do you think you're going? You don't move 'til the EMTs get here."

"Maybe one of them will be female. Think of all the attention you can suck up," Kelly, teasingly said, but when I caught sight of her face I saw something else. Concern, possibly?

"This is what happens when you sleep with trash," Marilyn whispered in my ear.

"W-what?" I slowly struggled to get some words out, but my cheeks were burning up. I glanced over at Kelly and she glanced back with a sad half smile, turning up her lips. I wanted to believe everything would be okay, but being placed on a stretcher and taken to the hospital, I knew it wouldn't be okay and I was the one to blame. The guilt of how I was treating Ja'Shay was overwhelming. I covered my face with my hands as they rolled me onto the elevator, knowing I would never forgive myself.

CHAPTER FOURTEEN

Roland

I turned the corner and the last person I expected to see was Trina. She smiled at me as soon as we laid eyes on each other. She turned away from Lynette and Kelly, who kept talking among themselves as if she was never standing there.

It had been less than twenty-four hours since our altercation and Trina was calling my cell phone non-stop, leaving multiple voicemails and text messages.

"Roland, it's Trina. I know you're mad, but I can explain. Please call me back." I screwed up my face in a frown as I listened to the message. I knew it was childish to dodge her calls, but the betrayal was too raw, and I knew if I spoke with Trina now I wouldn't be able to handle my composure.

I took a breath and continued toward my desk because honestly, I don't know what else to do. My heart was pounding and I was sweating. As if yesterday wasn't bad enough, all the shit I said to her, I knew I needed to apologize, but I thought I had another day to figure out how I was going to muster that without coming off like an even bigger dick.

I finally sit down, turning in my chair to jerk my chin at Sheldon in a half-assed hello.

"Oversleep?" Sheldon ask.

"Naw, half a day."

I sat at my desk, not caring what people thought about my being the center of the latest office gossip. Then the hairs on the back of my neck stood as the voice from the earlier message wore on me.

"I...um...I need to talk to you," Trina spoke nervously as she approached my desk.

I made sure no eye contact was made, as we interacted. "Look, can we not do this now?" I glimpsed Sheldon arching an eyebrow at me before turning away, knowing he hung on every single word.

"Could you just...give me a minute?" Trina asked, as she held up one finger, visually indicating her request.

I still kept my head down. "Okay, I get that, but this isn't exactly the place for us to be having that conversation," I said with seriousness in my voice.

Trina huffed, spinning on her heels and walking toward the break room. I groaned and let my head fall back against the chair, closing my eyes for two seconds before I lug myself up.

"Way to stay strong." Cynthia laughed with her back to me.

I cut my eyes at her as I got up to walk toward the break room.

Moving closer I saw Trina pacing back and forth, looking uncomfortable as all hell. The corner of her lips were turned up, her brown eyes flashed up to mine, and I couldn't shake the thought that I shouldn't be talking to her, but I walked in anyway and breathed deeply. *Here we go.*

"Okay, what's up?" I crossed my arms, still avoiding eye contact. "I don't owe you an explanation, but really, Trina, we're not about to discuss this here at work." I walked out the break room. I narrowed my eyes while turning back toward her. "Don't you think you've done enough?"

"I don't understand why you're so upset with me. I didn't do anything to you." As we stood in the break room, staring at each other, a sense of unease began to fill the room as I mentally replayed yesterday's events with Trina embarrassing herself on the production floor.

"Damn it!" Trina hissed, slightly tapping her foot on the floor.

I exchanged a confused glance with Veronica and was glad to know I wasn't alone in the confusion of Trina's dramatic entrance.

"Is everything all right?" Veronica curiously asked.

"No, no, no," Trina groaned, rummaging through her purse, grabbing her cell phone and began furiously flipping through it. "Can you give us some privacy?" Trina asked, as she turned toward Veronica.

I was so glad Veronica was present to witness Trina's craziness.

Trina froze for a few moments before she spoke, giving Veronica time to walk away. *"So I'm just another notch in the bedpost for you? Man whore,"* Trina spat, enthralled in her own thoughts, I guess, trying to come up with a coherent response.

"Man whore?" I replied, unable to say anything more.

I looked behind me as I overheard someone say, *"He always have females fighting over him."* I can't lie; I relished the attention given by the various women in the office. I've slept with a lot of the female population and as a result from sleeping with most of my female coworkers and completely avoiding them the next day, I've acquired quite the reputation of being a whore, which somehow never seemed to bother me, but apparently, this time was different.

"Okay, you need to calm down," I said, From the color that her brown skin was turning, Trina was burning up. Like a fool, I continue to speak. *"What are you talking about?"*

"I'm talking about the fact that you've been lying to me. I need you to say it to my face." Her facial expression was stone cold.

I shook my head. *"Say what, Trina?"*

"So now you're going to act like, you're not fucking around?" she yelled. With tears in her eyes, Trina shouted and screamed at me. *"How could you do this to me, to us? I'm not stupid. I knew what you were doing and with whom."*

"What are you talking about?" Now I was getting pissed off. I was completely in the dark.

"These text message!" Trina screenshots of the text message conversation between Desiree and me.

Me: *You were amazing Desiree. Can't wait to make you scream my name again.*

Desiree: *LOL. Can't get out of my head what you did to me yesterday! Thinking of you gets me so wet, keep touching myself when I think about it.*

Me: *Is that so, well I can't get the image of my dick sliding in and out of that tight, wet pussy of yours.*

Scrolling down the text messages, my memory rushed to catch up with the evidence. Damn, not only were there text messages, there was also a picture Desiree sent me a week ago. I spotted that butterfly tattoo above her left breast right away. There were no words. Nothing I could say. Taken aback, this was a bit much and I thought back to how I wanted to change before this type of thing happened. The messages, as well as the pictures, told it all.

Trina looked as if she had been crying for two hours. I handed the phone back to her without a word. I realized then I was approaching dangerous territory when it came to Trina. She felt a sense of ownership in my life, when in reality she had none. It was as if I had unknowingly put a ring on her finger and was disrespecting our marriage.

Trina sniffled and wrapped her arms around herself, glancing at the floor for a minute before her eyes dare to meet mine. And when they do, we're both staring at each other; my breathing was labored as my heart beat faster and faster. I wasn't sure where this was going and I was sick of her possessive ways.

I guess Trina called herself confronting me about sleeping with Desiree and with all these text message, she had me red handed. The entire time she was talking, I stood there shaking my head in shock. Then, I decided to man up and to stop the foolishness.

"Tell your husband he can have you back because I'm done with you." I knew my baritone voice bore down on her as I was now towering over her. *"You don't get to tell me where I go and who I fuck, Trina. Get over it."* There was a slight quiver in my voice, but calm and serious, so she would know I was not playing and, to make my point as clear as day, I snatched her phone and threw it in the trash.

"Who the hell do you think you are?" she shouted. *"Grow the hell up."* I could see how aggravated she was that I was calm and threw her phone in the trash.

"Trina, get out of my face. Your head is so far up your own ass that you can probably smell your shit." I chuckled and moved toward the door.

I grabbed the door handle and heard low sobs. I knew she was crying. I shouldn't have turned around, but I couldn't help but look in her eyes. The tears began flowing down Trina's cheeks when our eyes met. Shaking her head, she angrily began to speak.

"No, Roland. Not this time. I'm sorry...not me...not this woman...not my heart. This is a challenge I am not willing to take."

My only response was to glare at her before I turned and left through the break room door.

"*Roland!*" she screamed, as she jogged to catch up to me. "*Talk to me. Come on.*" She pulled at my sleeve. "*Roland, let me explain,*" she begged.

I yanked my arm free, refusing to look at her.

Trina and I began texting each other innocently for a while then it advanced to flirting all day long on Instant Messenger. Trina loved the attention and I gave it to her because I had feelings for her. Long story short, Trina proposed we start a sexual relationship because she wasn't happy at home. However, shortly after we began our sexual relationship, her husband found out and went ballistic. He hacked her voicemail and tried to confront me in the parking lot here at work. I couldn't risk any unsavory publicity because I had other females I was dealing with here at work. So, I ended the fling with Trina abruptly, cold turkey. That's until she came running back for more, which now I see was turning from bad to worse, real quick.

All my lies were catching up to me. As Trina stormed out of the break room, my first thought was to run after her, but my pride wouldn't let me. I'd done enough damage. Suddenly, I understood what I had to do. Reflecting on the start of my womanizing ways, I saw the details, saw all the events, saw it all again and felt it all connecting. I understood it now, so completely. I wondered why I didn't see this coming, even though I'd been warned many times before from Trina to Desiree, Chase,

Keisha, Patrice, the list goes on. Now I understood. I had to get shit together fast, or I was going to live the rest of my life alone.

CHAPTER FIFTEEN

Chanel

Locking my computer, I didn't think anything out of the norm of being called into Glen's office. It wasn't unusual for him to meet with representatives that reported to him directly or indirectly. Glen was my boss; he was one of the manager's in the Collections department. I went straight to Glen's office and lightly knocked.

The door swung open and my eyes fell directly on Kelly sitting in a chair directly across from Glen. The seriousness in her expression ruined my mood. I went from happy to angry and disgusted at that moment I realized this wasn't going to go as smooth as I originally figured.

"Please have a seat, Chanel." Glen pointed to the empty seat next to Kelly.

My eyes darted nervously to the vacant spot. I nervously sat down in the chair and with a shaking hand, pulled down on my shirt. I even went out of my way to scoot the seat closer toward the desk.

Before I could get comfortably seated, Glen didn't wait to get straight to the point. "We have to let you go."

"Wh…what?" I stuttered.

"Chanel, you were previously warned on your unprofessional behavior. During your probation period, in which we should have let you go, you received a verbal warning for being insubordinate toward your previous supervisor, Robin. Two weeks and four days after that you were placed on a written notice for the verbal altercation you had with another employee, Raven, in the middle of the production floor. The final notice came once you chose to dismiss company policy and exclaim to a customer, and I quote 'Bitch, if your bill was paid we wouldn't be having this conversation.'" Glen paused. "My last straw was how nonchalantly you peruse the Internet, no matter who's around you. You feel as though because you have a slight seniority here, that it gives you a pass to do as you please. I'm here to let you know that's over as of now."

The whole time Glen was reading off my list of infractions, Kelly sat there as if she were peering through my soul. She seemed as though she wanted to go down a list of things to say as well…once Glen was done.

I nodded, letting him know I heard everything he said. "I apologize, Mr. Adams. I promise you will see an immediate change," I pleaded, knowing we'd been down this road before.

"I've worked here for ten years, does that matter?" I said, feeling close to tears.

"You brought this on yourself," Glen nonchalantly said, looking at me with both disgust and pity.

"Are you fucking serious!" By this time, I had already jumped out of my seat running on pure rage, while my head began to pound. I took one last look around his office, placing my eyes on the nameplate that sat on his desk: Glen Adams. I wanted nothing more than to swipe all the papers off his desk and onto the floor. I was beyond pissed; my blinding rage was beginning to get the best of me and I wanted to punch this pasty face saltine in his face. Turning to face the door, I caught a glimpse of security posted up outside the office. So once I saw them, I knew they knew *I was the wrong bitch to fuck with*, so decided not to show them what unprofessional really was. I spotted Glen rubbing his thumb over the side of his facial hair.

He devilishly grinned as he ran two fingers over his mustache. I quickly adjusted my collar on the white button down shirt. I turned to face him, trying to figure out if I should say something or just leave at this moment. I decided to leave it alone.

"Have a wonderful day, Chanel. I wish you the best of luck." His words shot through me like fire as I looked up to find him grinning at me. I turned to face Kelly who had previously slipped out the office and was now standing behind me with my purse and car keys in her hand, and then I snapped.

"Are you serious?" I asked in the nastiest tone possible with a little neck twist, while snatching my items from her hands.

Glen narrowed his eyes at me and opened his mouth as if he were about to speak, but instead he smiled and rubbed his mustache for the third time. I had no desire to move.

"You know what? I ain't even gonna go in on y'all bitches in here. Oh and Kelly, you might want to remain quiet because your feelings will be left on the floor." I stormed out the office. I could feel Kelly glaring a hole in my head as I headed out the door.

Kelly rushed behind me so she could escort me to the door. I threw my badge in her face and hurried down the stairs toward the exit, feeling overwhelmed.

Hearing "We have to let you go" was the last thing I thought I would hear when I woke up this morning. I got fuckin fired from work today. I gave those assholes the best ten years of my life and they fired me! What pisses me off the most is that they knew they were going to fire me probably on Friday when I left work. So they let me have an amazing weekend just for me to wake up at six o'clock in the morning, drive thirty minutes to the other side of town, have me work for four hours, and then fire me.

What am I supposed to tell my kids? Having security escort me out of the building was embarrassing, and that bitch Kelly, with my desk packed up in a box. I stood in front of the building, staring at the front door. I was so overwhelmed with emotions, mostly rage. I'm known for going straight Puerto Rican on people, but instead I took the pictures I had on my desk from the box and slipped them in my Michal Kors purse and threw the rest of the shit on the ground next to the garbage. I didn't want any reminders of this stupid job that betrayed me.

I walked rapidly toward the parking lot, managing to avoid the puddles of water scattered across the uneven pavement. I sighed as I started the ignition and simultaneously reached under the passenger seat to grab the bottle of Wild Irish Rose. Glen Adam's words echoed in my head, banging as loudly as the pulse of my heart, "We have to let you go." I felt as if I was about to go crazy, my foundation rocked to its core. I began hyperventilating. I really felt as if I were near death.

"Shit!" I yelled, as I took a gulp of my liquor to calm my nerves as the corners of my mouth began twitching.

Chapter Sixteen

Desiree

I refused to cry, not in public at least and definitely not at work. On my drive to work, I played Marsha Ambrosius' 'The Break Up Song' as loud as I could. "Tears streamed down my face from all the emotions I was holding inside in regards to Roland, even though we were never officially committed to each other, I considered us to be in a serious but unofficial dating relationship.

"Come on, let's go to lunch and talk," Ahmad whispered in my ear. I nod as he linked arms with me and we began walking toward the elevator. "I can treat today. My direct deposit hit my account last night." He laughed

"I don't want your pity, Ahmad," I snap.

Ahmad rolled his eyes and sighed loudly. "Just let me pay for lunch, okay?"

"Fine, I'm getting a glass of wine, just so you know."

At the restaurant, were seated in a booth in the back. After we ordered and the waiter brought out a basket of bread, and my glass of wine, Ahmad finally broke his silence.

"So, are you okay?" He slowly buttered a slice of bread.

I shrugged. "Another man with his false hopes. I don't know how I'm going to manage coming to work every day and seeing Roland. I've done pretty well at avoiding him, but that's not going to last long." I took a long sip of wine.

"You know these niggas ain't loyal, but you can always transfer to another department if it's that serious."

I nodded and sighed. "Hopefully, it doesn't get to that point."

The waiter returned with our entrees. Spinach Lasagna for me and Shrimp Alfredo for Ahmad. We eat in a comfortable silence, me mainly because I'm depressed, but Ahmad, I'm guessing because he doesn't know what to say.

I broke from my train of thought when I felt Ahmad tugging on my hand, calling my name. "Desiree…." He looked at me strangely.

The anger inside me was swirling and expanding. Suddenly, I felt like I was choking on it. It became overwhelming how much I wanted to scream, cry, and take everything out on Trina for bringing this shit to me. It's not fair I know that, but focusing on my anger rather than the situation at hand was the only thing that kept me sane.

I gathered my composure and offered Ahmad a weak smile. "Umm, what's up?" I mumbled out, trailing off, my words getting stuck in my throat.

Ahmad shook his head; his smile faded a little when I met his eyes and nodded, sensing a significant moment between us. I smiled. "I'm sorry I ruined lunch."

My eyes were bloodshot and burning from crying so much. I hadn't moved from the spot I was sitting in for the last thirty minutes. Tears still trickled down my face, forming a puddle on my shirt collar. I didn't bother trying to stop. What was the point?

"He's a man. Let's be realistic. You were not the only one he was seeing," Ahmad bluntly said.

"That's complete bullshit!" I exhaled deeply. "This shit isn't right?" I raised my brow.

Ahmad's words pierced at my heart and made me weep out loud. Painful memories overwhelmed me, and no matter what I did, I couldn't stop them. Roland and I had a mutual under-standing and we didn't want our situation known to others. Too much trouble, too many complications. Everyone saw us as good friends, best friends even, and we both agreed it would be best if they didn't know otherwise. It had only been five months, but it felt like years. To forget all of that, to lose what we have now as if we never were...

"Listen, Dee, if you can't trust your partner, it's time to get a new one."

"I know, but I don't know." Tears were falling faster now and I felt my lungs constricting, making it harder for me to breathe. I knew if I didn't stop, I would send myself into a panic attack.

"I'm not supposed to say anything. I swore to secrecy, but if I tell you, you must promise not to say anything to anyone. Not even the parties involved."

"I won't tell anyone anything you tell me, I promise."

"Veronica fucked around with Roland back in the day. I don't know for how long or when. I just know it happened."

"Huh?" My heart was hammering away inside my chest. "My cousin?" I yelled. I didn't think this situation could get worse. Ahmad just gave me the most painful news. Not only was my heart broken, it also felt like it had just crumbled and dropped to my stomach on top of knife in my back. My face grew red. "How long have you kno—" I stopped talking. "Never mind, it doesn't matter."

"Please don't say anything," Ahmad blurted out before I could do or say anything else.

I cringed at the mental image Ahmad just put into my head. "I'm so fucking pissed right now! I cannot fucking believe this! This is like a slap in the face, but I promise that I won't say anything."

Ahmad and I drove back to the job in complete silence, aside from the radio. We ran inside the building, leaving behind the pouring rain. Ahmad rushed through the door first, twirling and flipping his dreadlocks trying to shake off the water. The door closed behind me, nipping my heels as Chanel stormed out the door.

While trying to make it back to my desk on time from my lunch break without fussing Chanel out for being rude, someone called out to Ahmad. We both turned around.

"Hey, Boo! I ain't seen you in forever." It was Kia, a Customer Service Representative who worked on the first.

"Girl, I'm just tryna maintain. Keep my head low, I'm tired of this place," Ahmad joked, but was dead serious.

Kia stood in front of us, viciously chewing on her gum while staring at the blue and grey New Balance classics Ahmad was wearing. "What size yo feet is, Boo? You got some big ones!"

I laughed hysterically, glancing down at his shoes.

"My feet are a size 12, but these sneaks are a 12½."

Kia flirtatiously replied. "Mmmmm, I know you packin' though....what that be like?"

Throwing the flirts right back, Ahmad replied, "Oh, girl! I'm holding quite well. My man is very satisfied."

"I bet he is...well you think you can handle all of this here?" Kia questioned while rubbing on her ass.

I stood there in disbelief, listening to this conversation before I casually walked away toward the stairs en route to my desk with Ahmad in tow.

Ahmad turned around with his foot on one stair and said to Kia, "Honey, this ain't what you want!" Both Ahmad and I laughed.

The two people I didn't want to see at the moment—Veronica and Roland—were standing at the top of the stairs, laughing and talking. I felt betrayed by both of them and things were certainly not going to be the same. I came to a fast conclusion that I would handle that situation if and when it came up. Besides, I might have wanted to fuck Roland again; I didn't know what the future had in store.

"Hey, Desi!" I felt a pair of hands on my shoulders as I tried to walk by but they blocked my path.

I stepped forward enough that Veronica's hands fell off my shoulder.

"Hey," I replied coldly.

Veronica looked at me with confusion. "I thought we were going for drinks last night?"

I gave a scornful laugh. "Nope."

Veronica turned to Roland. "Okay, I'm going to leave that alone. I will talk to you later, bro, by cuz," she said, walking away.

As I was making my way back to my seat, Roland snagged my attention as I tried quickly to pass him.

"Did you—" he whispered.

I cut him off. "What?" I cut him off, breathing hard from running up the stairs.

"They fired Chanel."

He took me by surprise. "Wait a minute. What! When?"

"Just now and I don't know, I just found out about it. Didn't get all the details." Our eyes read each other's, trying to see what we were feeling.

I immediately felt my stomach sink at the thought of talking to Roland. The extreme numbness that I've felt after our falling out over Trina and that text message fiasco had me feeling as if I was suffering from a suffocating illness. At work, he would send me instant messages saying he missed me and wanted me back, blah, blah, blah. Roland messaging me could have been a lifeline because I really had strong feelings for him, but the way he played games between Trina and me, I wanted to rip him a new one.

Roland was amazing; he was very considerate, especially in the beginning of our situationship. We had a connection and I knew this from the first time we officially hung out. I did two things most people wouldn't do on a first date: I got shit-faced drunk and I threw up in the parking lot of the bar. He stood by me and took care of me, and he never judged me.

He was patient with me, only kissing me on the cheek. It wasn't until three weeks into it that he had full on lip-kissed me. He had told me that he didn't want to be just a cuddy buddy, and I had agreed. While I had to admit in the beginning I was only using him to get my mind off my ex, Jason, and try to calm the numbness, I actually genuinely liked Roland.

Seeing Roland still hurt. As much as I would like to say I was over him, I wasn't... at least not completely. It had been unexpected when I had received his two texts the night before. I wondered what made him suddenly want to talk after we had spent a good two months avoiding each other like the plague. But,

I was secretly happy he was still thinking about me. As amazing as it would have been to have him back, I knew I couldn't… it wouldn't end well for either of us, and if I really had to admit it, I knew that within time I could actually come to love Roland.

"I'm not surprised she got fired; she's always had a nasty attitude. But thanks for telling me." I made sure to smirk so as not to sound rude as I walked away.

"You're welcome, sweetie," he slipped in while I was still in ear distance.

I turned around and we both exchanged understanding smiles. Everything within me screamed how wrong Roland was for me, yet I was going against my better judgment as this felt so right. Yes…he felt so right.

CHAPTER SEVENTEEN

Ja'Shay

My heart skipped when I saw Glen's name on my caller ID. This was the last thing I was expecting. I hadn't heard from him in several weeks. Arching my brow, I answered the call.

"Hello. Wow this is a surprise." I smiled. I couldn't help myself. I glanced at my stomach. A baby...a baby was on the way. I still couldn't get used to the idea of my being a mother. I was adopted at the age of six and now that I was becoming a mother, the thought had crossed my mind to try to find my biological parents.

For a while, my childhood was good. I had two wonderful adoptive parents. When I was thirteen, my parents divorced, and my mother took my sister and me away. We moved to Norfolk, Virginia from Memphis, Tennessee, and I was devastated. I missed my father. I was a rebellious teen toward my mother and I sought independence in any form. It hurt her a lot and I will never forget the pain I caused. So my wanting to give my child the best I could give, including having the father in the picture, was something I prayed about daily.

"I just wanted to ensure the baby was okay." Glen sounded so lost.

"Oh." I paused. "Yes, we're *both* okay. I've sent you updates via text message." I rolled my eyes. My smile vanished from my face. I wished he could know how devastated I had been.

There were a few moments of silence before Glen spoke again. "I've received them. I have to go. I will talk with you later." The line suddenly went dead. I breathed deeply and held the phone to my ear. I took another deep breath and tried to pull myself together. Closing my eyes, briefly I sighed. A few minutes later, I got a text message: *Sorry for bothering you. I wish you the best of luck with the baby.*

When I first found out I was pregnant I wasn't ready for the rumors or speculations so I hid my pregnancy by not telling anymore. As the months passed, I could no longer hide my growing tummy, so I began wearing maternity clothes and that's when the whispers and rumors began floating around the office. I was kind of relieved I didn't have to hide my pregnancy anymore because now I could finally be comfortable with my pregnancy at work.

I woke up the next morning feeling depressed and weird. I didn't want to go to work today. I didn't want to see Glen and I was tired of people asking me questions about my pregnancy. I sighed as I sat up in the bed. I walked over to my closet, picked out an outfit, jumped in the shower and I go through the motions of getting dressed. While brushing my teeth, I glanced in the mirror and cringed. I look like a Walking Dead extra. I forgo any makeup and after dressing in my maternity outfit that would make a nun beam with pride, I pulled my hair back in a half assed sloppy ponytail. I grabbed my Michael Kors purse and walked downstairs. I walked into the kitchen and grabbed an orange from the fruit bowl. Fighting back the tears, I head out the door to my doctor's appointment. How could I have been so careless and ended up pregnant?

I was twenty-four, and I had no relationship with my unborn child's father. When I arrived at the doctor's office and the nurse hooked me up to the machines to hear the baby's heartbeat, something didn't feel right. Until this very moment, I hadn't realized I hadn't felt the baby move all day. After the nurse moved the wand around for a moment, she returned it to its holster.

"I'll be right back," she said, leaving the room.

Dr. Wolk rushed into the room and started prepping me and ordering the nurses around.

"Dr. Wolk, what's wrong?"

"We can't hear a heartbeat."

Tears flowed down my face. "I don't understand, what are you saying?"

This has happened before, but not an entire day. Just two weeks ago, the nurse was showing me the baby on the ultrasound.

"There is your healthy baby," the nurse had said, pointing to the monitor. "Your baby now has her nose, fingers, limbs ears, eyes, and mouth." And now today, my baby didn't have a heartbeat, and none of this made any sense to me.

"We must deliver the baby soon. I need for you to go to the hospital right now and check yourself in. I will have the nurse call over and let them know you will be arriving soon."

I nodded as if I truly understood what was going on. Everything at that moment was a blur. After finding out that my baby had no heartbeat, I called my sister and asked her to meet me at the hospital. I debated if I should call Glen. He hadn't been around all these weeks and after the text message he sent me last night, I didn't see the purpose of calling him now. *Did I do this? Was this meant to happen? Is this a blessing?* Maybe I should have been more confident in becoming a mother.

Glen rushed to the hospital after my sister insisted that I text him. "Ja'Shay!" he hugged me after he walked into the room.

Surprised, I hugged him back as my eyes darted around the room then finally back on him. He walked over and sat next to my sister, April.

"Hi, Glen," April said softly.

I didn't take the time to introduce them considering how I was still pissed off at Glen.

"Hello. And you are?" He asked.

I lifted my head, pushing my hair back as I stared at Glen. He looked restless and scared. My eyes narrowed as April replied.

"I'm her sister."

I let out a groan and leaned back in my bed. I looked around the room and I saw something in Glen's eyes; something I hadn't seen since he went all 'white man crazy' on me. His grey eyes flared with intensity and I could tell he wanted to say something.

"Somebody please go get the doctor!" I yelled, as I banged on the bed rail.

"Ja'Shay..." Glen said, trying to stop me from yelling, but I shrugged him off.

"I said I need somebody now!" I yelled.

A short Black woman, with a bright red hair bun, made her way into the room and glared at me before reaching forward and stopping my hand before I could bang again. "Calm down, sweetie, we will have this baby out of you very soon."

"I need meds now!" I yelled at her. "And I want some goddamn answers right fucking now!"

She rolled her eyes, grabbed her clipboard, and looked it over. "Name?" she asked.

"Shay...I mean, Ja'Shay McPherson."

Her eyes got wide as she stared at the clipboard. She looked up at me with sad and surprised eyes before putting the clipboard back down. "Looks like we have a stressed baby." She tried her hardest to keep a blank stare, as all doctors seemed to have. "We're going to give you several doses of Cytotec to ripen your cervix."

I didn't give a fuck about any of that shit, I wanted to know about my baby. . "Will my baby live?" I asked, trying to ignore the hopefulness in my voice.

She looked at me blankly, but I saw the moment of sadness flash across her face. Then it was gone as fast as it came. "Chances are slim." She reached over to me and gently rubbed my arm. "I'm very sorry, dear." She pulled away, forgetting her clipboard as she walked away.

I didn't even try to hide the tears. This hurt; I never felt something like this. It was as if half of me was getting ripped away. By 7:00 pm, I had only dilated 4-centimeters, but my contractions were on top of each other.

"Apr—" I started but stopped when I heard the monitor speed up.

April looked at my eyes fearfully, obviously not knowing what was going on.

"Ja'Shay, what's wrong?" Glen asked. Almost immediately, nurses were rushing into the room. When the nurse couldn't find her heartbeat, I got scared.

"Is everything okay?" I asked. *Everything will be okay. Nothing is going to happen to my baby, not us. I just worry too much. It must be because I'm having contractions that they can't find a heartbeat. The doctor will know what to do.*

Then the doctor on duty came in with another nurse who was pushing the cart with the ultrasound machine. This was not going to be good, I could feel it. The look on the nurse's face was that of terror, which caused fear in my heart. The doctor placed the ultrasound gel on my stomach and pressed the wand on top of my large belly. Then she was on the screen, as she had been so many times before. But, wait, she wasn't moving. The place where her heart should have been fluttering was still. Her image on the ultra sound looked like a portrait. No movement. The doctor kept searching, staring at the ultrasound for what seemed like hours. I knew. She was dead. I knew.

"The baby's not going to make it," the nurse expressed

I began crying. My worst nightmare was coming true. The doctor walked out, but came back in a few minutes later and I asked, "What do we do now?"

"We deliver the baby."

I asked for a C-section. The doctor said no, that it wasn't in my best interest. I was shocked, angry, and at a loss. *This is unfair*, I thought. *I don't want to deliver her; I don't want to be awake for this. I don't want to go through this emotional pain. Who cares about the physical pain, just rip her out of me. You already told me my baby is dead, why do I have to suffer the emotional and physical pain of delivering her?*

Do something! Be useful, I was thinking. You couldn't save my baby, but maybe you could save me some pain and suffering. That was not the case. I would then spend the next six hours in labor. There is not going to be a birth. Just the delivery of a dead baby. They gave me an epidural and the next six hours were the longest of my life. To make matters worse, I had a fever that maintained at 103.9 for hours, even with them giving me antibiotics. I started to shake from the infection that I learned might have caused her death.

I started to worry about me. "Am I going to die, too?" I looked over at Glen and I could tell he, too, was concerned with this question that I had uttered out loud.

The time finally came when I was to give birth. The doctor came in with the two nurses; my sister and Glen were holding my legs. It was time to push. It was time for this nightmare to end. And then it happened. She was delivered. There was no sound. No crying, screaming, or movement. But she was here, all seven pounds eight ounces of her. They laid her on my chest, another moment when time stood still. She was beautiful. She had curly black hair, long lush eyelashes, soft chubby checks, a small button nose, big luscious lips, and pale skin.

CHAPTER EIGHTEEN

Kelly

I just finished solving a dozen problems and now everything was rolling smoothly, when suddenly, out of nowhere, I heard the distinct sound of a woman fussing. I stood up and followed her voice. I thought it was someone on my team arguing with a customer. I should have known from the high-pitched, annoying voice that it was Sheldon's girlfriend, Erica, being dramatic, as usual.

What the hell is going on here for God's sakes?

"Sheldon," I called out. I really didn't want to get involved at that moment; however, Erica and Sheldon were beginning to cause a scene on the production floor.

"No Sheldon, I don't want to hear that. You better not be lying," Erica said as she raked her fingers through her loosely curled weave, clearly aggravated. "I called you several times last night and your phone went straight to voicemail." Once again, she didn't wait for a response from Sheldon as she began wiping tears from her eyes. Erica was always tearing Sheldon down with her words and actions, and she claimed to be a good Christian woman when her actions clearly showed otherwise.

I closed my eyes and took in a big breath of air, then let it out slowly. I put on my serious face as I walked toward Sheldon's cubicle. "Erika, how are you? Sheldon, are you on break? If not, you need to keep company time to a minimum." I looked directly into Sheldon's eyes.

Erika chewed on her bottom lip, clearly upset. "I'll call you later, boo," she said with an attitude as she turned and walked away. Sheldon shrugged as if he didn't care whether she called or not. As Erica walked away, Sheldon and I shared a small smile as I stood in silence by his cubicle, but my ringing desk phone quickly interrupted it.

I turned back around as my phone stopped ringing. "What's wrong?" I asked Ahmad, immediately concerned with his silence.

"Nothing's wrong everything is peachy," he spoke with a smirk affixed to his lips.

"Do you remember our little team competition a few weeks back?"

"Yeah I remember. Jessica still hasn't collected her gift card." He smiled a little wider and nodded.

"I'm glad you reminded me. I will run out today and get the gift cards. But I need for you to create another contest to start next week, this time make it about most dollars collected." Ahmad nodded his understanding. "Make it fun, like last time."

Ahmad looked at me with a pause before replying. "I've got this."

I walked back to my desk to find Michelle, my gossip buddy, sitting in my cubicle.

"You would not believe what I just heard!" Michelle exhaled.

"What?" I held my breath, anticipating the slanderous news that might emerge from my best friend.

"Ja'Shay is pregnant with Glen's baby," Michelle whispered.

"No!" I exclaimed, as she nodded. "How did you find that out?" I looked around to ensure no one was listening.

"Ida in Customer Service is her manager. I guess Ja'Shay was having a bad day and needed someone to talk to, so she broke down crying and told Ida whom she was pregnant by. Begged Ida not to tell anyone, but of course Ida told me. You already know she's my peer mentor, so she confides in me a lot."

I shook my head. "Glen told me he and Ja'Shay were dealing with a little situation, but that's a major situation—" I stopped mid-sentence as I was startled by Jessica standing outside of my cubicle.

"Hey, Jessica. You need help?"

"Yes, I have this customer on my phone that's requesting a manager because he's not receiving his statements," Jessica explained

"Handle that girl; I will talk with you later." Michelle stood and walked out my cubicle.

"Now is not the time," I growl, throwing my muffin into the garbage can, as well as my cold coffee. I throw my hands up by my ears, as if I was surrendering. I laughed and so does Michelle. "Okay, I'll call you later."

I've been in management for about six years now and I've only managed phone agents. I like the challenge of being a manager as well as the higher pay, but one thing about me, I don't make up excuses for not meeting deadlines. I'm a '*worker bee*' to say the least. What I don't like is the excessive crap that comes from my employees. Sometimes I just want to slap the shit out of them.

My eyes were tired, so, so tired. Every flutter of my lashes made my eyes burn. I had forgotten my eye drops at home this morning and the pain from the constant glare of my computer screen made it worse. My fingers were sore, too. I've been working all day on my monthly performance reports. I was at my desk way after my shift ended, but these reports had to be on Glen's desk by tomorrow morning at nine.

"Has anyone seen Desiree? She's been in after call work for over thirty minutes," I yelled from my cubical.

"When I was coming back from break I saw her walk into the training room opposite side of the women's bathroom," Sheldon answered

"Training room? For what?"

Sheldon gave me a look letting me know he did not have an answer to my question.

I closed my laptop and walked toward the training room. When I approached the door, it was locked. I knocked softly on the door and was greeted by silence.

I put my ear up against the door to see if I could hear footsteps, and when I heard what sounded like someone tiptoeing around, I knocked three times. There was no answer, but I could hear what sounded like someone moaning on the opposite side of the door.

"John, do you know if Roland is still here to unlock this door?" Curiosity had gotten the best of me. I knew Desiree wasn't in there using her cell phone during work hours, which was surely a cause for a write-up.

"I'm not sure. I haven't seen him since earlier today. If you need to get in the room, one of the janitors can open the door. I think I saw the younger guy over by the fitness center."

"Okay, thanks. I will walk over to see if he is still there."

I located the janitor after walking halfway across the floor.

"Hi do you have the key to open the training room by the women's bathroom?"

He gave me an odd look. "I can only use the key to clean, and you have to call maintenance for that." He began walking away, dragging his cart of supplies.

"But you're right here, now," I responded. "But thanks anyway"

Chapter Nineteen

Desiree

I was sitting at my desk on my fifteen-minute break reading my favorite book *Wicked Attraction* for the thirteenth time when my cell phone buzzed, making me jump. I pulled out my phone to see who was texting me. It was Ahmad. His text read: *There go your boo*.

Suddenly a thought occurred to me as my stomach fluttered nervously. My fingers flew as I typed a reply" *I'm about to go talk to him, I miss him*. I pressed send and within a second, my answer popped up on his phone because I heard Ahmad's voice shout, "Get yo man." I turned around and met a pair of dusty brown eyes.

I waited about ten minutes before I started walking toward the training room. I had to come up with a plan because if I just showed up Roland would know something was up. I could make up a story, but he knew me too well to be fooled.

"Where you going?" Ahmad asked in singsong voice as I walked down the aisle.

"None of your business," I replied in the same tone.

"Oh, I bet you're going after your boo." He grinned like a teenage girl that knew a secret as he giggled.

"I'm actually not, I'll have you know," I lied

"Ohhh, how about your friend with benefits? Going to see him? Or her? I don't judge."

I scoffed. "Hell no! I'm not a lesbian!"

"That's what I said at first." Ahmad winked.

I scoffed once again, something I found myself doing a lot when I was around him. "Asshole," I mumbled.

"What was that?" Ahmad asked as he put a hand to his ear and leaned down, even though he obviously knew what I said.

"I said you're a fucking asshole!" I shouted loud as can be without being heard.

"I see." He nodded. "But I was just putting it out there. I mean, you and Roland are friends, right?"

I scoffed. "I'd hardly call it that."

"What would you call it then, Desi?"

"A... partnership. We're partners. In work. Don't you dare make a sexual joke about that." I chuckled. He so would. In any situation, Ahmad could make a sexual joke, no matter the circumstance.

I continued to laugh, and so did Ahmad. "So where you going?" Ahmad asked. "Just admit it."

"Who says I have to tell you where I'm going."

He looked at me, sincere but still goofy.

"Nobody. But I still want to know." He smirked.

"Ancient Chinese secret," I replied as I walk away

Adrenaline pumped through my veins as I poked my head into the room. Roland was sitting with his back toward me, working on the computer.

I admired him for a second before speaking. "Hey, are you busy?" My voice was shaky much like my hands as I closed the door.

"Not anymore."

When Roland looked at me, I saw the confusion that played out across his face, which I understood since we hadn't spoken much lately, other than an occasional hi and bye. And here I was, barging into the training room without any prior notice.

"What's going on, sweetie? I'm sorry, can I still call you that?" he asked with a guarded tone.

I put on a little smile, letting him know everything was okay. "Nothing just came by to say hi."

"This is a pleasant surprise." He stood to give me a hug.

A moment of silence passed between us, but I didn't mind at all. I could sit in a room with Roland, have no words spoken between us, and that would be enough to make me eternally happy.

"Aren't you looking nice today," Roland spoke, referring to my outfit. It's just my brown blazer over a low-scoop pink tank top and a pair of skinny jeans. "You should wear those jeans more often; they really bring out your nice butt." He winked at me.

My jaw was completely laxed and my eyes were wide, eyebrows totally and fully raised. As much as I hated admitting it, I missed Roland. We have a few things in common...actually, more than a few. We listened to almost the same exact music, we both loved basketball, amusement parks and blueberry muffins. If my future boyfriend didn't like blueberry muffins, it was not going to work. Definitely a deal breaker.

I remembered the day very distinctly, when I started to have a crush on Roland. It was the fourth day in my training class, but then as the weeks gradually went by, I realized it was just a really great first impression. I realized Roland was sometimes nice, but usually cocky, cute, and annoying, all at once. Like when we would insult each other. He was very clever, but so was I, which almost made us equals.

I moved closer to Roland and pushed him against the wall. There was nowhere for him to move. I pushed my body against his, feeling his hard chest against mine.

"What's the matter, Mr. Dumas? Don't you want me?" I asked in a soft whisper.

"Be careful what you wish for, Miss Bryant." Roland smiled, crossing his lips, and then I felt his thick lips pressed against mine. My lips met his earnestly, and I sighed as I felt his tongue brush over my MAC lip-gloss, my favorite: Dazzleglass.

Roland's tongue and fingers were a blur over my breasts now, working feverishly as he heard my voice tell him my secret fantasy. Then he moved back to my face, and kissed my delicate lips once more.

In a flash, I was on my knees in front of Roland. He didn't speak; he held his eyes closed tightly, struggling for breath as I sucked on his manhood.

"I know you want me. I've seen the way you look at me," I said in a lusty tone.

"Take off your pants," Roland ordered me.

He was now firmly in control of this situation. Although I'd instigated it, his authoritative personality was taking over. I had no doubt who was in charge. I loved it. I found the button of my jeans, and then I pushed the tight blue fabric over my thighs, down my legs, exposing my pink Victoria's Secret thong.

"Mmmm," I moaned under his expert attention to my most intimate of areas.

I felt his warm tongue rolling over my pussy lips now, and my eyes glazed over at the sensation. My body was shuddering as he carefully worked his warmth over my delicate chocolate folds. I felt his fingers spread them apart, and my whole body seemed to freeze as I felt his tongue probing inside my hot center.

"You like that?" he asked in a lust filled voice.

I looked at his face now, and could see his lips and chin glistening with my excitement. I nodded to answer his question.

"Yes," I managed to tremble out.

"What else do you like?" he asked me seriously.

"Umm..." I wasn't sure how to reply. I really wanted him to stop talking.

"Do you miss me?" he asked.

"Yeah..." I admitted, still breathless from his earlier exploration of my pussy with his tongue.

He smiled and then I felt his dick slide almost effortlessly into my tight, wet pussy. I gasped at the sensation. His dick was much thicker than I had remembered. I felt my walls allow him entry, and then hugged his dick tightly. He began to move slowly in and out now, and my eyes were glued open—unable to blink, as the sensations assaulted my body. The feeling as he fucked me was indescribable.

My body felt on fire, almost pulsing with desire with each gentle thrust of his dick; more and more of my pussy juice ran down my leg. Occasionally he would use his fingers to remove my juices, licking them off his finger. I watched dumbfounded as he savored the taste of my arousal.

"Fuck, Desi...you feel so fucking good..." he groaned.

Oh, God! My body trembled uncontrollably as I heard him cursing.

My body shuddered and trembled as Roland relentlessly pumped my tight pussy with his penis. He moved his face between my legs now, and I felt his tongue brushing lightly over my exposed clit as he continued his frantic licking of my quivering wetness. My sighs and moans increased under his expert attentions to my wanting body. I didn't care that we were at work.

"Oh, God…" I moaned, as my eyes rolled back in my head. The pleasure welling up inside me was ever increasing, my head rolled to the side now.

My body shuddered for a few seconds, and then I froze. My eyes locked wide open, and my voice was no longer working. I tried to scream, or moan in pleasure, but there was no sound. All there was…was pleasure. I have to get this man out of my system, he is so wrong for me.

Our fuckfest was cut short by a few knocks on the locked door and a couple of turns of the doorknob.

"Oh shit!" My heart felt like it was going to explode; I was so scared we would get caught.

"They can't get in. No one has the key but me and maintenance and they never come in here while I'm in here." Roland chuckled, aware of my fear.

I tried to get myself together, so I pulled out my wet wipes from my purse, along with my Bath & Body Works body spray, Beautiful Day, to try to conceal the smell reeking from my body. My nerves were shot to pieces after this. I needed a cigarette badly and I stopped smoking six months ago.

"You better hope none of your little friends didn't stay up in me," I joked, but was serious as we both gathered our breaths and put on our clothes.

I hurried back to my desk and no sooner than my behind hit the chair, I received an instant message. It was Ahmad.

6:44 PM Ahmad Mohammed: Hey whore

6:45 PM Desiree Bryant: Damn you! Don't call me that

6:45 PM Ahmad Mohammed: I just call it how I see it. That's what you call a woman who does nasty things like you do…lol

6:46 PM Desiree Bryant: I so dislike you…lol I can't wait for this day to end. I need a shower bad

6:48 PM Ahmad Mohammed: Yes you do, I smelled you when you walked past

6:50 PM Desiree Bryant: I'm sure you did because we got nasty…lol

6:55 PM Ahmad Mohammed: because you're a whore… call me when we get off so I can hear about all the nasty details

6:57 PM Desiree Bryant: I don't know if you're ready for these details. He must have really enjoyed himself because he's already texted me. Round 2 tonight

6:58 PM Ahmad Mohammed: I ain't mad at you; you better grab him up before I do

6:58 PM Desiree Bryant: I'll fight you before I let that happen

While I was messaging Ahmad, I checked my email, and there were two messages. The first was from Veronica and the second was from Kelly.

Desiree,

Efficiency is important to the day-to-day operation of our depart-ment. While we make allowances for extreme circumstances, consistent unauthorized time off the phone cannot be tolerated.

Today your phone was left in ACW (after call work) for over forty minutes until I had you kicked out the system. I checked and during that time frame, you were not at your desk. You logged out at 4:45p.m. for break and returned at 5:00 p.m.. The system did not show that you were scheduled to be off work early.

Should there be extenuating circumstances, please come and speak with me. If there is a problem, perhaps we can work it out together.

Please reply to this email with an explanation of your time off the phone between the hours of 4:35pm-5:20pm. I will also meet with you tomorrow to discuss this further

Thank you,

Kelly

Everything was always so dramatic when it came to Kelly and her management style. She was actually a very nice, intelligent woman, but sometimes I didn't like the things she did as a person in general. She was okay though. I didn't like her, nor did I hate her. I was always considerate of others, but I was really starting to resent her and her actions. She had a very loud voice. I thought she simply didn't think about it, but she yelled instead of speaking, and frequently put people down in front of others. My reply to Kelly's email was short and sweet.

Kelly,
I was in the restroom, sick.
Desiree

Chapter Twenty

Chanel

After being fired, I spent my days slouched on the couch, watching re-runs of *Martin* and drinking Crown Royal Apple. It was extremely depressing to realize just how much my life had changed over the course of a few months. I was not getting unemployment, so my bills were piling up. The child support from Elvin barely got us by. I had reached the fuck-everybody stage in my life, feeling like I was the only person in the world suffering. On an emotional roller coaster, my emotions were all over the place, from being shocked to being upset to being frustrated to being normal to not giving a fuck.

Ahmad called about an hour ago and said he was getting off work early and he was coming over to visit me. He was a good friend and I felt bad for avoiding his phone calls the last few weeks.

Ahmad was now knocking on my apartment door, but I ignored it. I just sat slumped on the couch, staring at the almost empty bottle of Crown Royal Apple in my hand. I was having second thoughts about letting him in. The lights were all off and most of the blinds were closed, so he couldn't see inside, but I managed to roll off the couch to open the door.

"Hey, whore, about time you opened the door. I've been standing out here for ten minutes." He marched inside and slammed the door. "Damn girl, Chanel, have you seen yourself? What happened to the diva that stepped into work every day? You're looking more like a troll." Ahmad burst out laughing. He had never seen me in this state even on my worst day— disheveled clothes, uncombed hair, eyes were red-rimmed and almost sunken, and my skin was pale.

"Shut up, Ahmad, I don't need your crap!" I picked up a few toys that my son had left scattered around the living room.

"Seriously, Chanel. Is that the kind of hello I get?" Ahmad rolled his eyes.

As I finished putting away the toys, I caught a glimpse of myself in the mirror. My dark brown hair was a mess, and I didn't have a stitch of makeup on. I smoothed out my hair before straightening out my shirt. It's not like I cared about what Ahmad thought. Well, I did. I didn't want him to think I was a stressed, even though I was. I walked over to the couch and sunk into the cushions.

"Hey, girlfriend, I miss you." Ahmad had a mischievous glint in his eye.

"I miss you, too, boo." I faintly smiled, pushing hair away from my face.

"Well, what's the 411, girlfriend?" Ahmad jumped right in, smiling deviously at his own question.

"Praying that Glen gets what's coming to him. His bitch ass pretty much told me to have a nice life, now get out my office."

"Well maybe karma got his ass because I heard that some girl name Shay or Ja'Shay, who works in customer service, was pregnant with his baby and she lost it."

"Shay…Shay. Umm, is she dark skinned, thin body?"

"I'm not sure who she is, but that may be her. All I know is she works in customer service."

"Damn that's messed up. I hate to say it, but that's what he gets for messing with other people's livelihood."

"Kelly is still being Kelly…annoying. She still doesn't know shit and all she wants to do is boss people around and embarrass them," Ahmad paused. "Girl, girl, girl, let me tell you what happened." Ahmad clapped his hands together. "Someone slashed all four tires of over ten cars, including Glen's and Kelly's cars, in the parking lot. It was hilarious because all we saw was tow truck after tow truck coming in and out of the parking lot. Rumor has it security turned over surveillance video or photos to the police and looking to press charges on whoever did it."

I began sweating. I looked down at the table as Ahmad was talking and my heart felt like it dropped. I was nervous and speechless. I slashed those tires and it wasn't ten it was more like four or five. I've never felt such rage inside me. I remember it like it happened yesterday.

It was a Wednesday morning, and I was having my worst day ever. I had just checked the mail and received notification that my unemployment appeal was denied, which meant the hole I had sunk into was becoming deeper. I could not control my anger any longer. I had snapped. I drove to Dollar General, purchased a box cutter and I went on a serious rampage. I wasn't quite sure how this was going to play out, but it was never smart for anyone to underestimate me, even myself. Better their tires than their throats, fucking with my livelihood.

"You okay, Chanel? You seem awful nervous." Ahmad rose from his seat to pour himself another glass of Crown.

I was shaken from my thoughts when Ahmad walked toward me, took my arm, and pulled me up from the couch, much to my persistence. "I'm good, just tired," is all I managed to say.

"Come on, get dressed. I'm going to take you out and get you some well-needed fresh air."

I rolled my eyes and sighed. Acting like a child, I stomped into the bedroom, groaning.

"Where are we going?"

As I was about to go into my story of why I was denied unemployment, there was a loud bang on the door. Then another, followed by, *"Police!"*.

I dragged my feet to the door and slowly opened it. Two police officers stood outside my door, and my heart immediately shattered.

"Chanel Serra?" the female police officer blurted, as the male officer stood watching.

"Yes, that's me." I offered a fake smile.

The female officer glanced up at me. "We have a warrant for your arrest." She handed me a piece of paper.

"For what?" I nervously asked as the male officer raised his eyebrow at me. I looked over at Ahmad and the look of horror on his face was priceless.

Ahmad stood up slowly as if he didn't really want to move. His movements were slower than his usual sharp pace.

"Sir, please stay where you are," the male officer ordered Ahmad.

"Vandalism and trespassing on private property," the female officer explained.

My eyes bulged and before I knew it, they spun me around and handcuffed me with extra, unnecessary force. "*You have the right to remain silent. Anything you say can and will be used against you in a court of law. You have the right to an attorney. If you cannot afford an attorney, one will be provided for you. Do you understand the rights I have just read to you?*"

I couldn't speak, so I nodded.

"Oh my, God! Oh, God! Oh my, God!" Ahmad freaked out. "Do you need me to call someone? Is there something I can do?"

Looking at him, I slowly nodded, with tears rolling down my face as the officers shuffled me out the door.

CHAPTER TWENTY-ONE

Roland

Every time the door opened and the cold air rushed into the room, I glanced up, hoping to see Desiree's face. It felt as though I hadn't seen her in years, instead of days. Desiree finally entered the break room, setting down the items in her hand. She huffed in exasperation as we made eye contact.

The low clacking of her high heels against the tile floor made me smile. She wore a grey pencil skirt with a pale pink blouse that had a ruffled collar. She donned her pink pumps and walked as if she meant business. I couldn't remember what my life was like before her, except I knew it was emptier. She made everything so much better. We were amazing together. The way she hummed around my dick and the vibration that ran down my shaft felt like an electric waterfall.

"You look very nice today," I slipped in as our paths crossed in the break room.

"Thank you, Roland." Turning around, she began walking away, but I called to her. The smell of her perfume was intoxicating. I touched her butt lightly as she turned around.

"*Oh my, God!*" Desiree roared. "You are such a child! You are a six-year-old trapped in the body of a grown ass man!"

I knew she was still mad at me, and she had every right to be. First the Trina situation and now Veronica. Before leaving my house a few days ago, she asked me what happened between Veronica and me. I couldn't lie to her, so I told her the truth. I told her it happened a few years back, but it was just sex that didn't lead to anything more. Veronica and I both agreed we would be better off as friends and both decided not to say anything else about it ever. It's obvious from what Desiree said to me that something was wrong and that the agreement between Veronica and me was broken. Based on the questions she asked me, I also picked up that she didn't find out this information from Veronica. But it was cool; we all live and learn.

I stopped Desiree from walking off. "Kiss me."

Her body stiffened. Turning around, she looked at me. The look on my face proved to her that I was serious. Desiree smiled, even though I knew she hated that I was talking to her. I knew she hated me for everything I did to her. Especially with Veronica being her cousin and neither of us spoke of our past history. "Glad I can assist the corners of your mouth to slightly curl this morning."

Glancing at the clock, Desiree rolled her eyes and turned on her heels. "You're such a jerk, such a fucking jerk," she said with anger fuming off of her like smoke as the door to the break room closed between us.

I knew things would never work out with Desiree. I haven't had many girlfriends. Commitments and I didn't really work out. For me, females meant just a fuck. How was I supposed to feel something else for…for a girlfriend? A relationship was built on trust. Trust wasn't a problem for me, but love. I had never felt real love. Maybe because I hadn't found the right person yet. Maybe because I didn't allow myself to feel love. Or, maybe I just couldn't feel it.

Desiree was beautiful, smart, and kind; her body looked perfect enough for me, her smile was downright dazzling. She was an amazing person from what I have learned over the last few months, so what stopped me from…from falling for her? I believed it was my stubbornness that made me not want to be in a relationship.

While it was great finally talking to Desiree again and things seemed to fall back into place as if it was just last week that we talked, when I sat back and truly examined everything, I concluded it was a treading of water going nowhere and would never go anywhere in the grand scheme of life. I would have been doing both of us a disservice holding on to something that in my heart I knew would have never manifested into anything substantial. Yeah, our sexual paths may eventually have crossed again, and I could make her spring a leak from that leaky faucet of hers, covering me in her womanly fluids or maybe she could treat my male friend like a popsicle on a hot sunny day when the temperature was one hundred degrees humid and melting fast, but after that marathon of excitement then what? I refused to change my lifestyle. I was a womanizer. I used women for sex and time fillers and that wasn't going to change until I was ready to change.

When I was younger, I used to compare myself to my father. We were both a lot alike, and I'm not just talking about looks; our personalities were pretty much the same, too. My father was cold and seemed rather uncaring; a selfish person, indeed, emotionless, with only a few people that could understand his behavior. So was I.

I really did like Desiree in my own, rather original, way, but I didn't love her. The way I talked to her, the way I treated her, the way my eyes would soften just at the sight of her; the way my voice was always warmer, calmer when addressing her. I didn't want to fall in love, at least not right now. People would do stupid things when in love, and I certainly didn't want that. I was a rational person, always putting my thoughts in front of my feelings. And I was selfish; what others thought or felt didn't concern me at all.

Unintentionally, I had learned a lot of Desiree's habits, and I knew how she reacted to certain things, how she behaved in certain situations. She seemed really kind, always putting others before herself. But even when I realized that, even though I had always wanted to meet a female like her—that would be interested in more than my money and looks—I forced myself not to care. Why? Once again, I had no idea.

A familiar hand, small and soft, rested on the base of my neck, fingers tangling in my short, raven hair, gently caressing the skin there. I looked in my periphery to see who was behind me. I braced myself as I spun around and was now facing Trina.

"Can I speak with you in private for a moment?" Her voice was shaking.

"Sure." I stood up and pushed my chair in and followed Trina.

She led us out of the break room and into the adjacent hallway. She stopped and turned around to face me. Several people smiled and waved as they rushed by.

"Should I be worried?" My voice lowered in concern.

"Hi, Roland." I looked up and waved to a girl passing by whose name I couldn't remember.

Trina raised an eyebrow at me, saying nothing. "Well, I have good news and bad news," Trina finally announced. "The good news is I'm getting a divorce." She smiled.

"Umm, okay, and the bad news?"

Trina hesitated. "I'm pregnant," she said, genuine regret tainting her voice.

Time seemed to have stopped for me. The unexpected news hit me like a ton of bricks, knocking the breath out of me and making my heart stop. My knees buckled, unable to support my weight anymore, and I fell back against the wall, eyes wide and lungs struggling to breathe. "What?"

"I'm pregnant."

"Don't fuck with me, Trina," I hissed, my worry spiking in all directions and manifesting, as always, into anger. "Is it mine?" I stated confidently, noticing how tired she looked.

"No!" she cried, tears spilling onto her cheeks as she squeezed her eyes shut. I can only imagine the pain she must be feeling that s she possibly lost everything that mattered to her.

"Hell, that may be bad news to you, but that's great news for me. Why are we even having this conversation?" At that point, I didn't even care. She could cry all she wanted and beg all she wished as long as she moved on with her life. I remained silent. There was nothing I could say. "You're not getting it." The words were out of my mouth before I could mentally process them.

"Good morning, Boo." Mariah, my friend with benefits, smiled warmly as she brushed past me. "Message me later, when you become available."

I nodded, acknowledging her request.

Trina angrily looked at me. "Getting what?"

"Another chance. We're done." It was almost as though everything was nothing more than a cruel joke, a message from God—a message that clearly stated that I did not need, or want, Trina around anymore.

Trina's jaw dropped open in spite of her grief. "Excuse me?" She blinked in confusion, raising an eyebrow. "And why the hell not?"

"Because I know I would regret it for the rest of my life," I answered completely honest.

"You're a selfish son of a bitch, you know that?" she snapped. "We have too much of a history together. We..." she paused, clearing her throat..

"We're not meant to be. Trina, you can't handle your emotions. Your husband confronting me at work, you were going through my phone, you confronting females about me at work. It's just too much," I said, avoiding eye contact.

Instantly, her eyes watered. It was over.

After talking with Trina, I found myself in a weird place. I instantly began thinking why a relationship with neither her, Desiree, nor anyone else would ever work, and I began sabotaging things in my mind. I went back to my desk and as soon as I sat down, I sent Desiree an instant message.

1:45 PM Roland Dumas: Ok, I need to say this; I think we should just be friends.

1:48 PM Desiree Bryant: All right, I'm a little surprised though, considering you know what happened recently.

1:49 PM Desiree Bryant: Well I was getting the impression you like me a lot even after the mess with you and Trina.
1:50 PM Roland Dumas: I do. I'm extremely attracted to you. You're very beautiful.

1:51 PM Desiree Bryant: Oh, well, thank you, so you don't like my personality?

1:52 PM Roland Dumas: No, I love your personality. It's one of your best features actually. I've been having a lot of fun with you. But I like you enough not to drag you along.

1:53 PM Desiree Bryant: I'm a little confused then.

1:54 PM Roland Dumas: I am too. I like you a lot, but I know I can't give you what you deserve.

1:58 PM Desiree Bryant: Well, all right. Feelings are feelings and that's fine. I have to say I've never had someone tell me they're so attracted to me and love hanging out with me and then reject me though.

1:59 PM Desiree Bryant: I guess maybe I want to move slowly with the next guy I see. Usually when things get exciting quickly they go downhill quickly too.

2:00 PM Roland Dumas: Yeah, I think we should just be friends.

2:01 PM Desiree Bryant: OK then, but it's gonna be hard for me not to text you special photos.. LOL. I'm going to miss spending time with you but I understand

2:02 PM Roland Dumas: Well... you can one more time. Just kidding. But I'm here for you as your friend. Have a great day buddy.

2:03 PM Desiree Bryant: You do the same buddy.

CHAPTER TWENTY-TWO

Desiree

For months, rumors of pending layoffs flew around the Call Center. Our conversations never focused on if it was going to happen, but rather when Human Resources would pay a visit with our walking papers.

The day finally came when a large man with a full belly, baldhead, and a thick British accent walked the production floor directly into the large conference room. Everyone was scared, there were whispers and a few people had tears pooled in their eyes, but no one really said anything. Hugs and kisses it was not. People just started gathering up their stuff and deleting personal computer files and e-mails, waiting their turn to be summoned into the conference room and handed individualized information packets explaining their severance packages.

Rumors have been floating around all morning that Human Resources released a list of positions to eliminate and the names of the managers who are being laid off, but the phone agents that were losing their jobs were clueless. I understood layoffs and change were a part of corporate life, but this whole situation was fucked up. I had to watch friends I'd grown to love lose a job and it didn't sit well in my stomach.

"The morale in the office is horribly low. How do they expect us to continue with business as usual with all this going on?" I asked to no one in particular. The axe hung over all our heads and no one knew where it would swing next. Those being laid off were being called into a room with Human Resources to say goodbye, told a few nice words, given a meager severance package of two months' pay average based on how long you've been working here, thirty days and then it was over. Today was going to be a rough one. Of course, if I'm on the list it was going to be a lot rougher.

"Right, if I'm on a call with a customer and they tap me on my shoulder, I'm going off. Fuck a payment," Ahmad said.

"I feel you," I replied angrily, my voice thick with tears, as I nodded. I cleared my throat. I couldn't focus. "Has anyone seen Roland?"

"I saw him earlier talking to Glen," Sheldon answered. I could honestly say that I was nervous and felt as if I was about to pee my pants. I took a bite of my bacon, egg, and cheese biscuit that I'd been nibbling on for the last two hours as I texted Roland.

Sometimes I got the feeling Roland hated me. Sometimes I got the feeling that he loved me. Sometimes I got the feeling that I hated him. Sometimes I got the feeling I loved him. My mind whirled at the course of his actions, and it made me want to punch him. I didn't like being confused, nor did I like being played with. Roland had a weird personality. I knew he had great qualities, but the majority of the time when he was around me, he seemed to be cocky, arrogant, and boastful, but around others, he seemed caring, sweet, and loving. I loved being around Roland when he was caring instead of arrogant and confident instead of cocky. That part of him was much more appealing, though. If he were like that all the time, I knew we wouldn't bump heads as much.

"Desi," I heard a voice say. I looked up and Roland was standing at my desk, glancing at me worriedly. I held up a finger for him to wait as I finished my call. I switched my phone into break mode and locked my computer, tossing down my headset. I got up and head down the aisle with Roland right behind me. I looked from the corner of my eye at Ahmad, who was currently on a call, but was now looking worried.

"How are you?" Roland asked.

"I'm good," I paused "Have you been in the conference room?"

"Naw, I honestly think I'm safe. From what I was told, they are getting rid of a lot of overstaffed departments. Customer Service got hit hard with a lot of layoffs."

"Did your girl get let go?" I asked, being sarcastic.

"Who Trina? Yup, she got let go. Veronica, too."

I gritted my teeth as a shadow of disappointment crossed my face. "Veronica?" Shocked by news I had never expected. "I can't believe my cousin got let go. Damn, that's messed up." From the moment I found out about her and Roland, I'd been very distant toward her. I had no reason to be mad because all of that happened before me, but I still expected her to tell me considering how close we were.

I had never seen greater incompetence in people skills than I had witnessed with this layoff. There was no trust in upper management or the corporate officers. It goes to show that no matter how productive you were or how good you may be, with a swipe of a pen from Human Resources, anyone could be let go due to restructuring. Treating people with integrity, honor, and respect will not only get the most out of them. Happy employees make great working conditions, which will make the overall job easier, especially during times of high stress or office emergencies. I was very surprised there hadn't been any acts of violence as of yet.

"I take it you haven't talked with Veronica?" Roland asked with a slightly raised eyebrow.

I really felt guilty and sad for not calling her and it would seem phony if I called her today. "Nope I haven't spoken with her."

"*What?* I just knew you would be the first person she told."

Looking up from the floor, my eyes and face were tearstained. "Nope," I replied with a hint of disappointment in my voice. "Should I call her since she hasn't called me?" I slightly shrugged.

"Why wouldn't you call her?" Roland confusingly inquired.

Suddenly I felt sick to my stomach, disgusted with myself and above all, I felt like I turned my back on Veronica for no reason. The thought alone was enough for me to run into the bathroom and throw up.

While we were talking, we heard someone crying. I peeked around the corner and it was Kelly. She ran to her desk, collapsed in her chair, and cried her eyes out. Both Roland and I were speechless and afraid to approach her. I was going say something to Kelly, but then I watched as Glen walked into her cubicle.

"Sorry about this, it's going to all work out," I overheard Glen say to her. "Take the rest of the day off and get yourself together."

I couldn't take the pressure, my anxiety level was rising, and I needed to talk with someone, so I walked up and pointedly asked Glen, to his face, if I should be concerned about getting laid off. He responded that I had nothing to worry about, but from his body language, I could tell he was lying and that he was uncomfortable about lying. I awkwardly walked away, still feeling uncertain. I turned around as I felt Glen's eyes scanning me.

"I've gotta get back to work, but I'll call you later," I said to Roland before walking off.

"Okay," Roland replied as he walked in the opposite direction.

I went home and even though I hadn't been laid off, I was in shock. I came into work the next day in a fog to find out that it wasn't just the rank and file. A vice present was terminated, so were whole groups from Customer Service, including department

heads as well as Kelly and a few agents from Collections. It was a
bloodbath. I was told that Rachel, who was in training with me,
vomited as she left the office for the day, that's how shocked she
was. Mark, the IT guy, was so shocked they said he sat in his car
in the parking lot for hours before driving home.

The next thirty days were the longest and shortest days thus
far in my career. This layoff changed a lot of individual's lives,
including mine. After Kelly was laid off, Roland was promoted
and was now my new manager. People around the office kept
saying Kelly got her karma for all the ugly and evil things she
had done to her employees over the years, but I didn't really
have a major problem with her. Ahmad's quitting came as a
surprise to me. One day, out of the blue, he texted me and said
he wasn't coming back because the job was too stressful for him.
He was planning on quitting a few months ago because during
his evaluation, Kelly criticized him for taking long lunch breaks,
unauthorized breaks, ignoring her emails, and being rude to his
coworkers and he didn't want to be walked out like they did
Chanel. I assumed after Kelly was let go, he would stay, but he
proved me wrong.

After the layoffs, I finally reached out to Veronica and we
were working our way back to where we once were. We didn't get
to hang out and talk as much as we did before, but now that she
and Ahmad were now working at the same insurance company,
I could have lunch dates with two of my favorite people. I saw
Ja'Shay, that Glen impregnated and she had lost a lot of weight.

She could get away with it on her body as she was so toned, but her face was so thin, her cheeks had lost all their plumpness and she had aged since the last time I saw her. I believed she had postpartum depression because every time I saw her she looked sad and hopeless.

I heard some new girl up here got Glen's nose wide open for right now. It would only be a matter of time before he was back to his old ways. Word got around about Chanel's arrest; some of the victims of her vandalism would be pressing charges against her, only because she had such a nasty attitude toward everyone. Even though we weren't on the best of terms, I still hoped she got the help she needed.

As I walked to my cubicle and got ready to put on my headset to start my day, I looked around the now scarce area and shook my head. This was the life of a Call Center and the internal affairs within.

ABOUT THE AUTHOR

Makenzi is an American novelist born and raised in Cleveland, Ohio. She is known for her true to life fiction novels: *Unexpected Truth*, *Wicked Attraction*, *Dangerously*, *That's How I Like It!* and the short story "Blood Brothers."

Makenzi has held various jobs in a call center environment in the corporate world. At the age of thirty, she decided to write her first novel, *That's How I like It!* and she hasn't stopped writing since. She lived in Virginia Beach, Virginia for several years and she now resides in Tampa, Florida, where she continues to write page-turning novels.

www.ingramcontent.com/pod-product-compliance
Lightning Source LLC
Chambersburg PA
CBHW021150130626
46554CB00005B/1745